My Name is....

Stories inspired by teens
of divorced, separated,
or single parent families

John Berrens

Gracednotes Ministries
405 Northridge Street NW
North Canton, Ohio 44720

My Name Is....
Stories inspired by teens of divorced, separated, or single
parent families

© 2022, John Berrens

Printed in the United States

ISBN 9798357052278

Dedication

I am humbled by the hundreds of students who had the
courage to share their family stories with me
over the last forty years.
Without them, this book would never have been written.

Introduction

This book is a compilation of fictional short stories for and about preteens/teens growing up in nontraditional families. They were inspired by the hundreds of students I have met in both group and individual settings. I have tried to create a diverse sampling of situations and challenges these families face. No story follows the life of any one individual. They are everybody's story, they are nobody's story.

When I started writing this book, my primary audience was young people growing up in separated, divorced or single parent environments. I wanted them to understand that they were not alone in their feelings or situations. Many of their classmates experienced similar hardships, fears, questions, and emotional ups and downs. They worried about their future and sometimes were haunted by their past. Even their views on marriage and relationships were challenged. But as I wrote, I realized this book was also for their peers that were growing up in more stable environments. While they may not identify with some of the situations, they certainly could identify with many of the questions and feelings. And more importantly, it was an opportunity to raise awareness and empathy, and maybe even create a network of support.

Friends and public opinion are everything to this age group.

The secondary audience is parents, helping professionals and teachers. Again, this book was written to create insight and raise awareness. This book is not meant to be critical of separated, divorced or single parents. Sometimes relationships have to end. Adults struggle with this impact on their lives as much as children do, but adults have a perspective of the situation which their children do not. Finances may be disrupted, living arrangements may change, logistics become a nightmare, and daily stress and emotional upheaval rise. This book can remind you to step back and see things through a child's eyes. Parent/child relationships can be tested in the best of times, but communication and honesty are even more important when navigating unknown waters. They will have questions, questions, questions, usually unasked, because they are afraid or unsure of how to voice their concerns. When possible, and appropriate, include them in the process of moving forward and finding solutions to the difficulties your family is facing.

JT

My name is John Thomas, but everybody calls me JT. I am thirteen years old, in the seventh grade with an eleven-year-old sister Terri. We just moved into our fourth foster home and my fourth school.

Where It Started

When I think back to my early childhood years, several words come to mind – crazy, unpredictable, and scary. In my opinion, my parents, Deloris and Jimmy, were parents in name only. They obviously knew how to make babies, but that was about as far as it went. My earliest memories have us living in some big building with lots of other families.

I don't know what Dad did to make money, but I recall him constantly complaining about work. He had to get up too early, stay too late, it was too hot in the summer and too cold in the winter. His bosses were all stupid, and he was never paid what he was worth. I think he changed jobs often. I don't know if he was fired or whether he just quit. No high school diploma for that wizard. Mom often complained that he could make more money if he would finish something called a GED.

Mom had worked at a fast-food restaurant and cleaned late afternoons at a day care center. There were other jobs, I just don't recall what they were. Mom complained about her jobs, but not like Dad.

Money, Money, Money

Money, or should I say not having enough money, or how money was spent, was a typical reason for a fight. Dad always yelled that they never had enough. Mom always complained that he spent it on stupid things. She nagged about him going out to the bar with his buddies and spending a fortune on pay day. He argued that it was his money, and he could spend it how he wanted. He complained that she should find a job which paid better. As time passed, their fighting got worse.

Strike One

One hot summer night, a lot of yelling and screaming woke me up. I put my ear to my bedroom door listening but was afraid to open it. They both yelled words I'd never heard before like, "dumb drunk, slut girlfriend, useless piece of shit, bitch" and more. Suddenly there was a loud bang, followed by mom sobbing as if she was hurt. Within seconds, the front door to our place opened and slammed shut. Mom continued crying. Dad had left and I didn't know what do. I wondered if she might be hurt. I crawled back to bed, too upset to sleep, but too scared to check on Mom. I stared at the ceiling for-ever. Terri remained sound asleep.

The next morning, everything seemed messed up and out of place. A lamp was missing its shade, magazines were on the floor, and a cushion from the couch was out of place. What had happened? Mom was sitting at the kitchen table with a bag of ice on her face. She glanced in my direction, shaking her head back and forth. I didn't know what to do. She obvi-ously had something wrong with her face and did not seem happy to see me. I heard Terri stirring in our room and was told to go get her and feed her. Terri did not appear to notice that anything was wrong. After breakfast I got us cleaned up and dressed for the day. I eventually got enough courage to knock on Mom's bedroom door to ask who was going to stay with us while she went to work. Mom yelled that she was not feeling well and was staying home.

Mom only left her room several times to use the bathroom, refill her ice bag, or get something to drink from the fridge. I tried to straighten up as much as I could. Terri eventually asked why Mom stayed in her room. "She's not feeling good," I told her. We got our own lunch and spent most of the day watching TV. Mom eventually came out around dinner time. Terri asked if she was sick. Mom said she was fine. One side of her face looked funny and was a dark color. Terri also asked what had happened to her face. Mom glanced at me while telling Terri she had tripped and hit her head on the nightstand. I believe she suspected I knew that was not the truth.

Dad not being home for dinner was not unusual. He stomped in the door as we were getting ready for bed. They looked at each other but said nothing. Dad had a big smile as he gave Terri and me high fives. I noticed that he smelled funny. That night in bed, I laid awake afraid of hearing more fighting. Luckily, all was quiet. The next morning Mom took us to our neighbor while she went to work. As we left, I noticed a bed pillow and a blanket on the couch. Wonder who slept there?

Strike Two

The problems between Mom and Dad only got worse over the next several months. One night, Dad came home, stumbled and fell over a stuffed animal that Terri had left on the floor. He blew up, yelled at Terri, who broke into tears as she ran to Mom. As he got up off the floor, Dad picked up the stuffed animal and threw it across the room. It knocked over a lamp, shattering the bulb. Mom was in his face – like now! It got loud real quick. She screamed, "You've been drinking again." Dad yelled that he was a big boy, and he could drink when-ever, wherever and with whomever he wanted. I didn't under-stand what this drinking thing was all about. He shoved Mom, who landed on the couch. He stomped out leaving the door wide open. I quickly ran to Mom, not knowing what to do. We cried. Mom was beyond angry. Dad did not return home that night. I was glad about that.

Within minutes, Taylor showed up at our door. She was a friend and sometimes babysitter from the apartment next door. She quickly figured out the situation and took us to the kitchen to get a snack while Mom cooled down. I could hear Mom and Taylor talking for a long time after we went to bed. I noticed Terri was sucking her thumb as she fell asleep. She hadn't sucked her thumb in a long time.

We spent the next day with Taylor while Mom went to work. When Terri fell asleep, I asked Taylor what Mom meant when she yelled at dad for "drinking." She explained that there were "big people drinks." If you drink too much, they might make you act different. Beer, wine and whiskey were big people drinks. I knew we had beer in our fridge. Was beer bad? No, as long as you didn't drink too much at one time. I wanted to know if Dad drank too many big people drinks. Taylor just smiled.

Dad was home when Mom got back from work. We hadn't seen him home this early in a long time. He was all friendly with everybody and even brought a cake for dessert. Terri was thrilled to see him. I wasn't sure. Dinner went okay. He volunteered to do the dishes. That was weird. Mom didn't exactly welcome him home, but rather appeared kind of nervous. There was no yelling after we went to bed and no pillow or blanket on the couch the next morning. The next several days went about the same. Dad was home for dinner and Mom gradually relaxed.

Strike Three

The next several weeks seemed to go okay, but I guess all good things come to an end. Dad wasn't home one Saturday when we left for a birthday party at Aunt Marissa's and Uncle Aiden's house. He arrived well after the party had started and was really loud, joking with everyone. He gave me a big hug, and I remember he had that strange smell again. He started arguing with Carl, a friend of Uncle Aiden's. Dad pushed him into the small wading pool. Carl was furious as he got out of the pool yelling that his cell phone was ruined and that Dad was going to have to pay for a new one. They started pushing and shoving. Others jumped in the middle to break it up. Dad stormed off as Carl yelled, "Drunks aren't welcome at family parties." There was that word again, drunk. Mom was inside when the fight occurred, only coming out as Dad was leaving. Aunt Marissa took her back inside. She wasn't the same the rest of the day.

Dad arrived home shortly after Terri and I went to bed. He was loud. An argument quickly erupted. We were both still awake. Mom called him a "useless drunk." He screamed that she was a "sexless bitch." The yelling went on for what seemed like forever. I heard their bedroom door slam. Mom must have locked it because he pounded on the door yelling for her to open it. There were several loud bangs. Mom screamed. Terri came to my bed and started to cry. We were trembling but had no idea what to do. The yelling continued. Suddenly, we heard pounding and yelling from the front door. It sounded like our neighbor, Taylor. We heard Dad go to the door, yelling at Taylor before leaving.

We slowly came out of our bedroom. Taylor embraced Mom who was crying. I noticed their bedroom door was broken.

6

Within minutes, the police arrived. The police, why were they here? Officer Tina sat down with Terri and me at the kitchen table. She was really nice. She asked a few questions about what had happened. Officer Tina also wanted to know if we had ever seen Dad and Mom get into any big fights in the past. Had Dad ever hit us, or Mom? Officer Brad sat in the living room with Mom and Taylor. When they left, Mom took us both in her arms on the couch. I didn't notice it at first, but she had a bruise over her one eye and a little blood under her nose. Taylor stayed.

Mom took us over to Aunt Marissa's and Uncle Aiden's house on Saturday. I should mention that they were the only relatives I knew. I've come to learn that Aunt Marissa and Uncle Aiden were our only family that lived in this part of the country. I sometimes have wondered why Mom and Dad never talked about or traveled to visit our family. We'd never even met our grandparents. The adults talked in the kitchen while we played outside. Something was up, I just didn't know what. Mom left with Uncle Aiden, returning for dinner. On the way home, Terri asked if Daddy would be home tonight. Mom did not know. I kept thinking about Officer Tina's questions. Mom had a black eye and there had been blood under her nose. Did Dad... no, he wouldn't do that, would he?

The bedroom door had been repaired by the time we got home. Still no dad. I was relieved, he was starting to scare me. The memory of Mom's bruised cheek and ice pack from several weeks ago came back to me. If he hit Mom, he might hit

Terri and me. I thought more and more about what Officer Tina had asked.

We spent Monday with Taylor while Mom worked. Dad was there when Mom got home. Terri did not seem happy to see him. Dad tried to get me to play a video game, but I really couldn't get into it. Mom kept her distance. Terri followed her around like a lost puppy. Nobody talked much.

You're Out!

Fall arrived and I was excited to start first grade. Mom's new work hours had her out several nights a week, so Dad was home with us on those nights. Things worked fine for about two weeks until one night when he wasn't home when it was time for Mom to leave. She called his phone but got no answer. She eventually called in sick, which was a lie. I never heard her lie before. She'd always preached the importance of telling the truth at all times.

I woke when Dad got home. I guess Mom had locked the bedroom door again because I heard Dad pounding and yelling. Eventually he gave up, slamming the front door as he left. Luckily, Terri slept through it all. I was scared but relieved that he was gone. I wasn't sure if I ever wanted to see him again.

The following week, Dad made it home in time for Mom to leave for work; however, Mom accused him of being drunk. His temper flared. Yelling started. I took Terri's hand and

8

headed to our bedroom. It went on and on. Mom came to our room, telling us to get our coats because we were leaving. I guess Taylor wasn't home. Dad sat on the couch, continuing to call Mom names as we left. We got to the car, and Mom realized she had forgotten her keys. We waited forever for her to return. I noticed that her hair was a mess, and she had been crying when she got back. Mom took us to work where Aunt Marissa picked us up. I missed kindergarten the next day.

The next morning, I noticed that Mom had some sort of brown thing wrapped around her wrist with a bag of ice on it. What was this all about? Mom said she hurt it at work. Later in the day, I overheard her telling Aunt Marissa how Dad threw her into the wall. It all fit together. I had to ask her. Mom broke down telling me what really happened. She was sorry she lied. I don't know why she didn't tell me the truth earlier. This lie was easy to forgive.

I hated Dad! What had he done to Mom? What might he do to her next time if he came back? How could any of us feel safe? He was a monster! I didn't ever want to see him again him. I now realized he had caused Mom's other injuries, and I wished I had told Officer Tina. I felt a little guilty. Maybe she could have kept Mom from getting hurt.

Necessary Changes

Terri and I stayed with our aunt and uncle for several days. They took me to school and watched Terri. I really didn't understand any of it, but Mom had gone to the police to tell them what had happened. We eventually moved back home. Mom told us that Dad wasn't allowed back in the house. The police had brought him to the apartment to get his things while we were out. That was the best news I'd heard in a while. Dad scared me. He'd hurt Mom several times, and I feared that he might get mad and hurt Terri and me too. I was beginning to understand what the word drunk meant. Why would anyone drink if that's what happens?

There were lots of changes over the next several months. Mom and Dad divorced, and she found a job where she could make more money. We moved to an apartment closer to my aunt and uncle. Dad was allowed a supervised visitation one time a month. He complained about having another adult present. The whole thing was weird and uncomfortable. Neither Terri nor I wanted to see him. We complained but Mom told us that he was our dad and we had to visit him. I didn't understand. He was a bad man. Why did we have to visit him?

Some Never Learn

Mom was in the bathroom one Saturday when there was a knock at the front door. We had been taught to never open the door to a stranger, but I recognized Dad's voice, so I opened it. I quickly realized my mistake. Dad was acting crazy, yelling he had every right to see his kids whenever he wanted. "Where is the bitch hiding?"

Mom quickly came out from the bathroom telling us to go in her bedroom and lock the door. Things got out of control

10

quickly. Mom's phone was on her bed, so I dialed 911. By the time the police arrived, Dad had left. Mom was laying on the floor with her eyes closed, not talking. She was bleeding from her forehead. An ambulance took her to the hospital. I gave the policeman my aunt's name which he found on Mom's phone. Aunt Marissa and Uncle Aiden arrived shortly. Aunt Marissa left for the hospital, while Uncle Aiden took us to their house.

Mom spent three nights in the hospital. We weren't allowed to visit. I overheard my aunt and uncle talking about Mom having a brain injury. What was that? I wanted to ask, but I didn't. I think I was scared of the answer. Mom wasn't herself when she was released to her sister's house. Several times I wasn't sure she even recognized us. She slurred her speech and struggled to find words to talk. She wanted to sleep all the time, and I don't recall her smiling for at least a week. Mom was like one of those zombies from the movies. We spent over a month with my aunt and uncle. Everyone, including the policeman who stopped by, convinced Mom to do something called "filing charges" against Dad. He ended up in jail.

I was scared, angry, and confused. I hated Dad. He had hurt Mom, which resulted in a trip to the hospital, but now he was in jail. Wasn't jail for bad guys, like bank robbers and murderers? Was Dad like one of those bad guys? I swore I never wanted to see him again, but I wondered if he was in jail because I called 911. Was I responsible for Dad being in jail? I was all mixed up!

Mom, Are You There?

I remember even after we got home, Mom talked less and often ignored us. Mom seemed unhappy, occasionally displaying fits of anger and rage. She never hit us, but we were scared. She called in sick to work more frequently. She spent lots of time in her room. She was less interested in seeing Aunt Marissa and her friend Taylor. They both tried to get her out shopping, to a movie or a restaurant, but she displayed little interest. I was getting worried but didn't know what to do. Mom rarely picked up around the house and seldom cooked a meal. Terri and I sometimes ate cereal for dinner. Mom grew kind of skinny, which was not surprising since I rarely saw her eat.

School

I was happy to start second grade. The summer had not been much fun. Terri and I were pretty much on our own. I packed my own lunch and got myself up in the morning. Several times I missed the school bus and just stayed home. My teacher, Mrs. Duebber, seemed to take a special interest in me, asking questions about my home. One day, she got in the middle when several kids teased me about my lunch, which included a handful of plain crackers and a cookie. Another time I was teased because I wore the same shirt to school all week. I didn't understand why I was being made fun of. At one point, a classmate gave me the nickname "stinky." I began to dislike going to school. I felt there was no good place for me to be.

Sometime after Christmas, I was called to the office to see Mrs. Draper, our principal. There was a special lady, Ms. Cramer, who she wanted me to meet. Mrs. Draper stayed with me while I spoke with her. At first, I was nervous, but Ms. Cramer was very nice as she asked lots of questions about my family. Who cooked meals, did the laundry, and cleaned the house? Was there food in the house? Was Mom home when I got up for school? Did Terri and I ever get left alone? Had any adult ever hit me or touched me in way that made me feel uncomfortable? Did Mom have a job? What kind of fun things did we do with my mom? Although I didn't understand who Ms. Cramer was, or why she asked so many questions, it sort of felt good talking to somebody about my family. Ms. Cramer indicated that she wanted to meet Mom. I only knew Ms. Cramer for a short time, but I liked her and thought it would be cool if she met Mom.

That evening, I told Mom that a nice lady named Ms. Cramer from school wanted to meet her. Mom wanted to know what it was all about, but I really didn't know. She was already home from work with Terri when I got home from school the next day. She was not in a good mood. Ms. Cramer had stopped by. Mom was furious about why Ms. Cramer was "in her business." After dinner, Aunt Marissa stopped over and I could hear them arguing. I couldn't understand much, but I did hear the name Ms. Cramer several times. I liked Ms. Cramer. How could they possibly be fighting about her? Nothing made sense.

Ms. Cramer stopped over about a week later when we were all home. She was still very nice. Terri took right to her. Mom was not happy to see her; however, for the rest of the school year Mom started doing a little bit more for us. She sometimes helped me with my lunch, cooked more meals, and was even awake to get me off to school. However, the unhappy cloud continued to follow her around. She still wasn't like our old mom. I worried more all the time. I think I'd become Mrs. Duebber's favorite student. I didn't mind her occasional questions about my family.

Summer, to Fall

That summer, Mom gradually drifted back into her old habits of doing less "mom duties." Aunt Marissa and Mom had several big fights. At one point right before the start of school, I heard Aunt Marissa bring up Ms. Cramer, which resulted in Mom going ballistic. We saw Aunt Marissa and Uncle Aiden much less after the blow up. One Saturday they came over to our place to tell us that they were moving to a different city for Uncle Aiden's job. I really didn't understand why someone would move for a job. All I knew was I soon began to miss them. After several months, I asked Mom if we could visit them. Mom said they moved far, far away, and we'd have to take an airplane to get to their house. Visiting them never came up again.

Several weeks after the start of the school year, we moved to a small building with four apartments. The new place was not very nice. It was on a busy street, and we had no place to play outside. I was mad that I had to change schools. Terri had just started kindergarten.

The new school was all right, but I missed Mrs. Duebber. Mrs. Castle, my new second grade teacher, was friendly, but I still felt like an outsider. Mom's unhappiness, anger flares, and lack of doing much for us only increased. Now I was getting both myself and Terri up for school and packed two lunches with whatever we had around the house. Sometimes we didn't have clean clothes for school. Terri always wanted to show Mom what she had done in kindergarten, but Mom showed little interest. She was often late picking us up from latchkey. Meals were usually heated up in the microwave. We usually got ourselves to bed. As the school year progressed, I thought back to how things had gotten better for a while after Mom had met with Ms. Cramer. Should I try to contact Ms. Cramer? How would I do that? I found myself getting angry at Mom. Sometimes, I felt like I was doing more to run our house than she was. I was only in the second grade! I wanted my mom back. Mom wasn't the only one who was unhappy.

Ugly Winter

Dad was released from prison after several months. I only knew this because I overheard Mom talking to someone on the phone. All I knew for sure was that I feared him and prayed I'd never see him again. One day, we got home from latchkey, and Dad was sitting on the steps leading to our building. Mom froze. Terri looked terrified as she grabbed Mom's hand. Dad was all smiles when he saw us. He looked different, with a full beard and a shaved head. Mom told us to get back in the car. Dad yelled that he only wanted to see his kids. She angerly screamed that he had given up his rights to see us. Mom said something about a police order for him to stay away from us. I knew nothing about what a "police order" meant. She told him to leave, or she'd call the police. He didn't move, saying he had served his time, and she couldn't keep his children from him. Mom quickly got in the car and we left. Mom's hands trembled on the steering wheel. Tears rolled down her face as she mumbled to herself. I didn't know what to do. I was mad at Dad and was frightened for all of us. Memories of him hurting Mom flooded my brain. I thought he was gone from our lives. I had a sick feeling all evening long.

Things got uglier over the next several weeks. Dad showed up at Mom's work. Her boss called the police, but he left before they arrived. He even showed up at school one afternoon telling the school secretary that he was there to pick us up. Luckily, he was sent on his way since his name was not listed as an emergency contact. The school called Mom and she contacted the police. She was not only unhappy, but she became more emotional and out of control, having no patience with anybody or any situation. Mom repeatedly told us never to answer the front door, especially if we recognized Dad's voice. She was nervous to even answer her phone. Before she had sort of ignored us, now, she yelled and picked on every little thing. Sometimes I just wanted to go to sleep and never wake up. I kept telling myself that I had to be there for Terri. I found myself thinking more about how I might reach Ms. Cramer.

Things had not been good for a long time, but now with Dad out of prison, it had gotten worse. I hated being home in the evening after latchkey. Mom's emotions were all over the place, yelling about this, complaining about that. Other times, she might be down in the dumps, spending hours in her room. I started having nightmares. In some dreams I just sat there while Dad hit Mom. Other times he dragged Terri and me to a car and drove off. I was not getting enough sleep and was occasionally caught dosing off at school. I struggled to complete schoolwork. I even got into a big yelling match with a classmate at recess over dodge ball.

Mrs. Castle tried to contact Mom for a conference, but Mom did not return her calls. She put a note in my backpack which I gave to Mom, but she ignored it. One day, Mrs. Castle asked if I could help her after school, saying she would take me to the cafeteria for latchkey when we finished. She asked about my home life and family as we worked. I soon realized that Mrs. Castle was acting a lot like Mrs. Duebber, who I really missed. Over the next several weeks, Mrs. Castle kept me after school several times, where we talked while she helped me with schoolwork. I eventually told her about Ms. Cramer.

One day, I was called to the office and much to my surprise, Ms. Cramer was there. I was happy and relieved to see her. We spent a long time talking. She was really interested in how Terri and I were doing. She appeared concerned when I described the change in Mom's behavior. I told her how things had gotten worse since Dad was out of prison. She did not know he had been released.

Once again, Mom was not pleased when Ms. Cramer stopped by. There were several visits over the next couple of months. They spoke while Terri and I went to our shared room. Things had gotten better when Ms. Cramer visited the first time over a year ago. Sadly, nothing improved this time. If anything, life got worse. I began to wonder if I ever should have said anything to my teacher. I had a hard time concentrating on anything at school or home. I looked forward to my weekly after school tutoring with Mrs. Castle. She really seemed to care. Terri started to lose her excitement for kindergarten. Home was the pits. Life was the pits.

Down the Rabbit Hole

Winter turned to spring and Mom's down moods seemed to be more frequent and last much longer, even though we had not heard from Dad in months. Mom missed more days of work, and we usually took care of ourselves, even though she was home. Ms. Cramer continued to call Mom and occasionally visited. We hadn't seen Aunt Marissa and Uncle Aiden since they moved, and I couldn't tell you the last time Mom's friend Taylor was around.

One afternoon Mom failed to pick us up from latchkey. Phone calls were made, but she didn't answer. Eventually, the police were called. I didn't know what to think when they put us in back of a police car to ride home. They pounded on the door, but she did not answer. The police got a key from the manager who lived in the building. No Mom. Terri, who initially thought the ride in the police car was cool, started to cry when they couldn't find Mom. I tried to remain calm, but tears welled in my eyes. Where was Mom? Was she hurt? Had Dad come by and taken her? Where were we going to stay if she didn't come home? Scared, worried, confused, upset ... I was overwhelmed!

Officer Tammy sat with us and got us something to eat while her partner made phone calls. She was really nice as she tried to assure us that things would be okay. Eventually, there was a knock on the door. Terri's eyes lit up as she yelled "Mom's home!" How could that be? Mom wouldn't knock, she had a key. Enter Ms. Cramer. Her familiar face brought a smile to my face, but where was Mom? After a few phone calls, Ms. Cramer told us that we would be going with her. She helped us gather a few things before we left.

I didn't know what to think. Ms. Cramer told us that we would be spending the night with a special family who helped out when kids needed someplace to stay. I didn't get it, "special family" – what was that? It was dark by the time we got there. Marge and Ken Metz greeted us at the door. Marge took us to the kitchen for a snack while Ken spoke with Ms. Cramer. They had a small black dog named Cinder who distracted Terri. We spent a little time talking with Marge and Ken before they showed us to our room. What was going on? They seemed okay, but why did they take two strange kids into their house? How long were we going to stay with them? How did Ms. Cramer know these people? Were we going to school the next day? Where was Mom? Was she safe? Were we ever going home? I didn't sleep much that night. I had an upset stomach again.

Ken took us both to school and was there to pick us up at the end of the day. At school Ms. Cramer told us that we would be staying with the Metzes for several days. We asked about Mom. Nobody gave us much information. I was more distracted than usual. I wasn't really thinking about anything but was sort of in a daze. Everything had happened so fast.

After spending three nights with the Metzes, Ms. Cramer sat Terri and I down for a chat. Mom apparently was in the hospital. She was not very specific in what she told us about her. She merely said Mom was currently unable to care for us, and we were going to stay with the Metzes for a while. Ms. Cramer hoped we'd be able to visit her soon. The Metzes were old and kind of strict. I laid in bed every night wondering about Mom, wondering about us, wondering about our family. Why did this have to happen to us?

After about a week, Ms. Cramer asked us if we wanted to see Mom. She took us to a place she called an "adult care home." She described it as a house where several women who needed a little extra help lived, before they returned home. What did Ms. Cramer mean by "a little extra help?" I asked but didn't get much of an answer. I was more than a little anxious as we entered the house. Terri immediately yelled, "Mom!" while running to hug her legs as she entered the living room. Mom did not hug Terri back, but sort of just stood there, expressionless. We made eye contact and it was like she was looking right through me. Our visit lasted around a half hour. Ms. Cramer tried to keep a conversation going. I remember feeling guilty about being relieved when it was time to go. Mom had not been herself ever since she ended up in the hospital due to a head injury caused by Dad. Now she was even weirder. Was she even happy to see us? Who knows? Would she ever be able to take care of us again? I began to have doubts. What did that mean for Terri and me? What was going to happen to us?

As it turned out, we spent the last few weeks of the school year with the Metzes. I didn't dislike the Metzes but it wasn't home. We continued to visit Mom once a week, but nothing really changed. It was like she was present physically, but not mentally. I missed weekly after school tutoring with Mrs. Castle which ended because Ken picked us up right after school. I was still having a hard time at school. It wasn't that I couldn't do the work, I just couldn't – I don't know, get into it – concentrate. I was still having trouble sleeping. I couldn't get excited about anything back then. Every time I asked when we would be returning home, I got the answer "hopefully soon." Did anybody know what was going on?

Summer Break

We returned to our apartment shortly after the end of the school year. Luckily, Mom's employer kept her on despite the last several months. At first it was nice to get home, but things were no better. Ms. Cramer kept in regular touch with our family, and Mom went to something called "counseling."

I also noticed that she had three pill bottles on the bathroom windowsill which I had never seen before. Mom was just out of it. She never smiled and didn't even get mad at us anymore. It was like she wasn't even there. Didn't she love us? If she did, why did she act this way?

Mom didn't pick us up from day-camp at the local church one day after work. This brought back memories from latchkey. The lady running the day camp had Ms. Cramer's number as an emergency contact. She took us back to the apartment where we waited for Mom, who never showed. Ms. Cramer, tried to act like it was not a big deal, but I could tell she was upset. After a number of phone calls, she told us we might have to spend the night in a "special house" again. It was a new family, the Kellys.

One night turned into several weeks. Mom had still not turned up. I was beginning to fear we might never see her again. The Kellys were a lot like the Metzes. We had a place to sleep and three good meals a day. They weren't mean, but they weren't very friendly. I became more unhappy and angry. I'm not even sure I knew who I was angry at. Was this our future? Every several months Mom disappears, and we live with strangers? I wanted to see Mom again, but in some ways I didn't. I just wanted things to get better. I wanted to be happy again.

No Show, So Moving On ... Again

Mom never did show up. Ms. Cramer tried to sound positive as she told us that we were moving from the Kellys to a "long term foster home." Neal and Donna Durban were introduced as our foster parents. I didn't get this "foster parent" thing. Parents? They weren't my parents. What did "long term" mean? Were we ever going to see Mom again?

We each had our own room which was a first. Initially, Neal and Donna had lots of rules. No clothes on the bedroom floor and no food in our rooms. There was a strict bedtime routine, with showers only three minutes long. Donna turned out to be a good cook; however, you had to finish everything on your plate, or you got no dessert. At the time I couldn't say I hated their house, but I couldn't say I loved it either. I continued to have trouble sleeping at night, spending hours wondering about Mom and what was going to happen to us next. Were we going to be with the Durbans forever?

School Year

Moving in with the Durbans meant a new school for third grade. Donna and I met with the school counselor where some of my personal and school history was discussed. I was sad to leave Mrs. Castle and some of my old friends. Obviously, I knew no one. Luckily, some of the boys invited me to their lunch table.

The new school was much tougher than my old one. They did things in math I'd never seen before. I was expected to read every night, keeping a daily log for Neal or Donna to initial. I had much more homework than I ever had in the past. There were some really smart kids in my class. As the year progressed, I felt dumber and dumber and fell further behind. I had never felt this way at my other schools. After Thanksgiving I started going with a student from a different class three time a week to work on reading. Even though the reading teacher was very nice, I hated being pulled from class to see her. I felt like I had a spotlight on me every time I left class. Mrs. Cassidy, my third-grade teacher was okay, but she wasn't like Mrs. Duebber or Mrs. Castle. Despite the extra reading help and daily assistance at home, I just couldn't get into school.

After Christmas, our school had a special day called "Mom's Morning." Donna came for Terri and me. I had not told any of my classmates that I had foster parents. At lunch several of my friends who sat with us for the program asked why I called her Donna, and not Mom. I tried to explain she was my "foster mom." I told them my mom was very sick and couldn't care for us. I guess that was sort of the truth. I didn't tell them anything about my dad. I remember feeling embarrassed. Another way I was different.

I barely passed third grade. The school counselor, Mrs. Conner, got involved early in fourth grade. She asked lots of questions about my real mom and our home life. I really didn't know this lady and did not truthfully answer many of her questions about my past. After several weeks, Mrs. Conner asked me if I was happy. I lied, rating myself a nine on a ten-point happiness scale. I don't think she believed me. I think Mrs. Conner knew more about my history than she let on. I guess she knew I wasn't always truthful.

That next several nights, I thought about my talks with Mrs. Conner. I slowly began to question whether she was right. Maybe I wasn't a nine on the happiness scale. Was I more like a three? I believed my poor grades were because I wasn't very smart. I continued to see Mrs. Conner twice a month. She became okay, but I still kept stuff from her. I'll give her this, she was pretty good at reading my mood within seconds of me entering her office. The best part of seeing her was getting out of art class.

Mom was always on my mind. I was mad at her for abandoning us, but I worried about her safety. Was she even alive? Did she ever return to the old apartment and find us missing? Wouldn't she have looked for us? Would she have even cared? Wouldn't she realize that she could have found us by getting in touch with Ms. Cramer? I didn't know how I felt about her anymore.

Time Moves On

Even though Neal and Donna had lots of rules, I know they really cared for us. We went on a week-long vacation to a small cabin resort on a lake the summer between fourth and fifth grades. Terri and I had never been on a vacation. It was maybe the best week we ever had! There was boating, fishing, hiking, swimming, bike-riding and a nightly campfire. No reading, math, writing, no studying for a test, no school! I never wanted to go home. I began to wonder if this was what most families did. What had Terri and I missed out on all those years living with Mom and Dad? I tried not to think about our past but instead tried to focus on the life we had with the Durbans. As good as it was, sometimes I'd found myself haunted by thoughts of my past.

I started playing both soccer and basketball at school. Although most of my teammates and coaches knew I lived with foster parents, it didn't seem to make any difference to them. I was just another kid. Everyone treated Donna and Neal like they were our real parents, which in ways, they were. Neal and Donna became involved in both Terri's and my school activities and teams. Terri even started taking dance lessons.

Even though life at home was good, school was, well you know, it was school. I did what I had to keep my grades passing, but there weren't any subjects I really liked. My school counselor continued to check in around once a month during fifth and sixth grades. We usually just played a game while we talked. I grew to like her; however, I knew she couldn't change what had happened in the past. No one could.

One day in sixth grade, two boys who I didn't know, started spreading a rumor at school that I was a foster child because my real parents were drug addicts. Some friends came to me at recess asking if it was true. I was furious with the rumor starters and was hurt that some of my better friends asked about it. A big fight broke out. Three of us ended up in the principal's office. Parents were called.

I was scared to go home that night, knowing I had let Donna and Neal down. Memories of my dad screaming at and beating my mom filled my head on the bus ride home. Much to my surprise, there was no yelling, we just talked. Much of the conversation centered around my past and how Terri and I ended up in foster care. They talked about their concerns for me. They truly cared about Terri and me. I got a punishment from both home and school but that was okay. I had screwed up.

Even though the fight was in the past and I was cool with Donna and Neal, the whole foster care thing was always lurking in the back of my mind. Why was my dad such a bad person? I'd never heard of any kids who had a parent who spent time in jail. There was never any yelling at the Durban's. I couldn't in my wildest dreams imagine Neal hurting Donna.

What happened to Mom? Sometimes I had to tell myself that she didn't try to find us because she was dead. But then, the thought of her being dead also freaked me out. I knew the Durbans cared for us, maybe even loved us, but they weren't my real parents. Sometimes everything was just too much. I got better at handling it when asked about foster care by kids at school. I didn't know any other foster kids from my school with whom I could talk or identify. I found myself experiencing more periods of unhappiness and loneliness.

Sadness

Sometime in late October of seventh grade, Terri came running in the house screaming that Neal had fallen while raking leaves and he appeared unconscious. Donna immediately ran out to investigate. Within seconds, she was calling 911. The ambulance arrived and they were off to the hospital. She sent us to a neighbor's house where she would call as soon as she knew something. Donna never called. Several hours later she came home telling us that Neal had died of what they believed was a heart attack.

The next several days were as bad as when Terri and I were abandoned by Mom. The usually cheerful, positive, take charge Donna was beside herself. Family members and neighbors were around offering help. I felt like I was lost in a dark cave of sadness.

After Neal's death, life was never the same at the Durban's. Within several months, Donna started running to this or that doctor with a variety of health concerns. Her grief seemed to overtake every aspect of her life. To this day, I still get choked up when I think about how sad Donna was. Even Terri, who was generally upbeat, wasn't herself. I tried to assist more around the house, but it didn't seem to help the overall mood. I found myself frequently thinking about Neal. Even though he wasn't my real dad, I realized that I had begun to count on him in that role. Neal was Dad.

Foster Four

Several days before spring break, the now married Mrs. Cramer-Fisher came to visit. We would be moving to a different foster home within weeks. Donna was moving in with her daughter due to health issues. She repeatedly expressed her love for us. Everyone cried. I know you're thinking, a seventh-grade boy crying? Well, it was just too much for me. Donna apologized over and over, but I knew it wasn't her fault. Even though she was moving to a different town, we promised to keep in touch. That night in bed, I admitted to myself that I had come to love Donna and Neal more than I realized. I think I secretly dreamed they would have adopted Terri and me. Maybe that's why it hurt so much.

Within two weeks, we packed our belongings and were off to a new place to live, our fourth foster placement. Terri and I were enrolled in new schools.

Again

So that's my story. Dad, a drunk, beat my mom, spent a few months in jail, and disappeared shortly after his release from prison. Mom had some kind of brain injury and I guess experienced mental illness. She eventually abandoned us, never to be seen again. I have many mixed feelings towards my real parents. Sometimes I hate them, other times I feel sorry for them. Are either of them alive? If they are, do they think about us? Terri and I were lucky to have Mrs. Cramer-Fisher to look after us. I think Terri would agree that the Durbans had become our family. I miss them terribly. When I'm in a down mood, I worry that I might end up like my dad or mom. I don't sleep well at night and school is well … school. I've come to recognize my unhappiness as depression. Mrs. Cramer-Fisher is setting me up with a counselor outside of school, which is probably a good thing.

I guess Terri and I will just have to see what's around the next corner. Can it possibly be any more crazy, unpredictable or scarier than our past?

Mia

My name is Mia. I'm writing this because my parents are divorced. I am currently a senior in high school and can't wait to move out and head off to college. My youngest sister Gail is in the eighth grade, and Megan, my oldest sister is in nursing school and lives with her boyfriend.

Mom moved out the summer between first and second grade. The kids stayed with Dad. Mom went with ... I'll fill you in more about that a little later. So, there we were, me starting second grade, Gail was a toddler, and Megan, a freshman in high school. You heard me right, three girls and Dad. He had no idea what to expect.

In The Beginning ...

As the story goes, Mom and Dad met at a party in September of their senior year of college. They came from different cities to attend the "Big U," as Dad always called it. To hear Mom, Dad fell hard for her. She had been dating another guy at the time, but Dad just wouldn't give up. After two months, Mom gave in and they went out. It was fun, but she didn't have the hots for him like he did for her. By Valentine's Day it changed. They were a couple. After graduation Mom moved to a city where she took a job as an assistant costume designer at South Creek Theater. Dad went back home, which was five hours away. Mom laughed telling how he drug his tired ass on a ten-hour round trip almost every weekend to see her. By spring Dad moved. They were engaged several months later and got married the next year.

I can't really say I recall any bad memories from those early years. Dad worked as an accountant. Mom sometimes called him "Mr. Number." I didn't get the nickname then, but I do now. Mom quit her job after she had Megan but returned part-time back in the costume department when I started pre-school at age four. All-day kindergarten meant a full-time job at South Creek Theater. Then along came Gail in late spring of my kindergarten year.

Looking back as a senior in high school, I often wonder whether Gail was an "oops baby." That doesn't mean she wasn't loved from the start, but that seemed to be the point when things started to get bad between our parents. It was obvious that Mom loved being back to work full-time. I kind of think Mom worried she might have to quit her job again.

Opposites Attract?

Dad was just Dad. He couldn't help himself back then. Mr. Number was often kidded about being so serious all the time. He liked things neat, orderly, predictable. When we went somewhere, he planned everything to the minute. He stressed over our disorganized, cluttered bedroom. Dad was also the family discipline guy. You didn't want to make him mad. He never hit us, but he yelled like a wild man when he was really angry. Many hours were spent at work, especially right after Christmas, which I learned was "tax time." Although often exhausted, he was always a good guy. I think he really tried to roll with a house full of girls.

Mom was not like Dad. Kicking our clothes to the side as she walked in our room was all that ever happened, as not much bothered her. Last minute outings with just us girls to parks, museums, and the zoo happened a lot. I loved those days. Sometimes we had no idea where we were going until we pulled into the parking lot. Mom rarely raised her voice at us, but when she did, we knew she meant business. How did they ever get together in the first place? A rigid accountant and the creative, carefree theater person, hmmm ...

Work Brings Changes

Mom loved being back at South Creek. Even when she only worked part-time, she often helped with extra things leading up to a production. That caused more stress at home. She occasionally got a babysitter for me after school because she had extra work. That was okay with me, but Dad did not like this one bit. Dad believed her responsibility was to be with the kids until we were in "real school," (translated, first grade). Mom argued that she loved being with her girls but needed something more for herself. The part-time opening in the costume design department was a rare opportunity that she couldn't pass up. No way she was going to turn down a full-time position when I started kindergarten. I really didn't understand all this fighting. I just wanted them to stop!

Dad became moodier as he struggled with Mom working full-time. Mrs. Schmidt, a neighbor, watched baby Gail. I stayed in latchkey at school when Megan was busy. Mom's work hours weren't regular and included way more evenings. Dad complained about take-out dinners when Mom wasn't home. I sometimes missed Mom, but what I really missed was them getting along.

During February, South Creek put on *Harvey*. Mom got tickets for everyone but Gail. For weeks leading up to the play, she talked about the costumes, the set, the great cast and how much she hoped we'd all enjoy it. It was "tax time," so Dad claimed he was just too busy to attend. I don't recall an argument, but I could tell she was hurt. Mom, Megan, and I had a great time. I didn't understand everything about the play but watching Mom's excitement was enough for me. Afterwards, Mom introduced us to several of the actors and the head costume designer, Laura. They all seemed to really like Mom. I'd never seen Mom so happy and proud. Dad was in his office when we got home. He looked up saying we'd better get to bed, or we'd fall asleep at school the next day. Dad did not ask anything about "*Harvey*." Didn't he care? Didn't he notice how happy we were as we entered the house? Didn't he see how important this was for Mom? What was his problem?

Summertime brought more challenges. I mostly stayed home with Megan, unless she had things planned with her friends. Sometimes I hung with a girl down the street from my class and occasionally a neighbor helped out. Gail, being an infant, continued to stay with Mrs. Schmidt. The schedule changed from day to day. Dad hated it. He needed to know where everybody was at all times. Arguments happened more often and got louder. Mom had a big outdoor production running for several weeks at the end of July. The teen theater workshop which South Creek Theater ran every summer also took her time. Mom was busy, but she loved it. Sometimes I got to go to her work. That was way cool. She was in charge of lots of stuff, especially with the teen group. Mom was like a teacher helping teens design and make many of their costumes. I thought Mom was great!

Mom got tickets for us to see the teen production of *Godspell*. Dad showed no interest. He didn't say much, sitting there expressionless during the whole show. How could anybody sit still during *Godspell*? The songs were so lively. There was a standing ovation at the end. Dad stayed seated. I knew that was wrong. I grabbed his hand and tried to get him to stand up. Nothing! Mom suggested ice cream after the show, but Dad complained he needed to get home to get something ready for work. I don't know the specifics, but there was a lot of yelling coming from their bedroom that night. What was happening? I was starting to get worried.

Mom looked exhausted the next day as we ate breakfast. Megan came down a few minutes after Mom left. Nobody knew what was going on. We'd never seen Mom and Dad like this before. Megan felt that Dad was being a jerk. Mom stayed home with us kids for years and finally was back to doing what she loved and had been trained to do. I didn't exactly defend Dad, but I wasn't as critical as Megan. I didn't know what to think. Their arguing had gotten worse since summer. I loved them both but … I just wanted things to get back to the way they were. I was starting to feel scared. No, I was scared. Where was this headed?

About now you are probably thinking about going back to the first several paragraphs to see if you got something mixed up. At this point Dad looks like the villain in this story. No, your memory hasn't failed you. I said us girls all ended up living with him.

The Final Year

The start of first grade does not bring back many great memories. Sure, it was cool to be at big kid's school, but our home had become a mess. My parents fought more and more. Maybe just getting out of the house was the best part about returning to school. They became less secretive about their growing dislike of each other. Dad sometimes made nasty remarks about Mom in front of us. It was like he was trying to get us on his side against her. Unfortunately, Mom sometimes did the same thing. Megan complained to me that Mom cornered her and ragged on Dad. It was like she looked to her as a friend who she could unload on, and not as her daughter. I can't say for sure about Megan, but I felt caught in the middle.

I didn't love either one of them more than the other. As the school year wore on, I found myself disliking many things about both of them. I began to feel guilty about my bad feelings towards my parents.

Thanksgiving, Christmas, and New Year were not joyous occasions. Neither sets of grandparents lived close to us or each other. In past years we had alternated between grandparents for Thanksgiving. We always saw both sets of grandparents sometime between Christmas and New Year. It became obvious to our grandparents that things were not wonderful in paradise. Mom tried to put on a happy face. Happy, really Mom! Dad didn't appear to give a crap. Mr. Number was more than just a little moody. We girls had been living with this for months. Our grandparents had obviously been kept in the dark by their kids. They quickly recognized something was wrong. Even cute little Gail couldn't change the mood.

We were with Dad's parents for several days between Christmas and New Year. I recall being relieved when Grandma asked me to go with her to the grocery store. It got me out of a tense house. Sitting in the parking lot before we headed back, she turned to me and said she noticed that neither Mom nor Dad seemed very happy. That's all I needed. We sat in the parking lot for a long time as I opened up to Grandma. I have to say Grandma was cool. She didn't take Mom's or Dad's side. There were no criticisms. I don't recall her asking hardly any questions. She just listened. After I was all talked out, she leaned across the seat and gave me a big hug. Grandma didn't say anything stupid like, "It will be all right." She just hugged me tight.

Nothing much changed around the house for the next several months. It was tax season, so Dad wasn't around a lot of evenings or weekends. That lowered the tension level. I guess that old saying "out of sight, out of mind" holds some truth. Mom was very busy, working lots of evenings also. Dad complained. However, where was he? Out doing tax stuff! I liked when one of them was working in the evening, less fights.

After the spring run of *Oklahoma* at the South Creek, Mom called the kids together to tell us that she'd been offered a new job. Dad wasn't home, but she'd already told him. She had the possibility of being a head costume designer. We all wanted to know what happened to Laura, the head costume designer whom we'd met many times before. The job wasn't at South Creek Theater. It was at the Monroe Theater in another city. I didn't understand, how could she work in a different city? Megan got a panicked look on her face. Were we moving? What did Dad have to say? Mom didn't have many answers. The new position started in June. If she accepted the job, she would be moving there by herself sometime in May. We were speechless. Mom tried to assure us that nothing was final and "everything would be okay." Easy for her to say! Nothing ever seemed okay anymore!

Megan and I headed to our bedroom. She suspected something was up for weeks, noting that Mom had toned down her fighting with Dad. Megan brought up divorce. Mom had not

38

said anything about divorce, but how could we remain a family if she lived hours away? Even though things had been bad for a long time, the idea of them splitting up never crossed my mind. All sorts of questions erupted. Where would we live? They wouldn't split us girls up, would they? Did any one of us really want to move to an unknown city? How would we keep up with our friends if we moved with Mom? Even though she had been working now for several years, Mom still did most of the house stuff. Did Dad even know how to grocery shop, do laundry or cook?

It would be so embarrassing to tell our friends if they divorced. I wonder if Dad even cared that she might be leaving? If we stayed with Dad, how often would we get to visit Mom? If we moved with Mom, how would we fit into a new school? We wouldn't know anybody! Would she buy a house or rent something, like an apartment? Would she even have room for us when we came to visit? How could Dad deal with three girls if we stayed with him? He'd been having more issues with Megan lately. Would that get worse? He just didn't seem to have much patience or understanding of young girls. We knew how busy Mom was as an assistant costume designer. Would she have time for us as head costume designer if we lived with her? We got more emotional, the more we talked. "Maybe they will stay together." Megan looked at me, then the floor. I don't think she believed that was going to happen. I again broke the silence, "Do they care about us anymore?" I started to feel sick. I was awake all night.

Several weeks later Mom and Dad told us that she was taking the new job at the Monroe Theater. She planned on leaving Thursday night to look for a place to live and hoped to return Sunday. We sat in silence. I can't come up with words to describe what I was feeling. My stomach started churning and I felt a little dizzy. I stared out the window trying to keep it all together. I think I knew something like this was coming but had worked very hard for days to keep it out of my mind. They both talked about how they hadn't gotten along for some time, suggesting that time apart might actually bring them back together. This made no sense to me at all. How can being apart bring you back together? We were staying with Dad for the time being until they worked things out. The word divorce was not mentioned, but I can assure you, it was on my mind. Sometimes it seemed like that was the only thing on my mind.

Bye ...

The next several weeks were really strange. The arguments between Mom and Dad ended. They pretty much went about their business in preparation for her move. At times there was an unnatural silence around the house. No one seemed happy, but no one said a thing. I wanted to scream!

Mom moved on Saturday, May 22nd, about a week before she started her job. Her parents arrived early, taking us in their car to see Mom's new city and apartment. Gail stayed with Dad. The four-hour drive seemed like eight. Our grandparents tried to keep the mood light, but I'll tell you, that was a tough order. Mom and Uncle Chad got there before us with a

40

pick-up truck filled with her stuff. The apartment seemed small, but nice. After the truck was unloaded, her brother headed back home. We headed off to the Monroe Theater where we met a co-worker Ben, who gave us a quick tour. It was time for the four-hour drive home. We all broke down. Even Grandpa had watery red eyes. It had happened. Mom and Dad no longer lived together. I ate nothing when we stopped for burgers on the ride home. My heart felt empty, as I stared out the window. I was exhausted, but I couldn't sleep.

First Months Apart

To say things were crazy is an understatement. Dad piled a lot more responsibility on Megan. I'd only just finished first grade and could not be left at home on my own. Megan never complained about having to watch me. Dad ran around like a hyper-nut each morning getting Gail ready for Mrs. Schmidt. He wrote stacks of schedules and lists, and Post-it notes were everywhere!

Household chores also changed. Megan helped with laundry and weekly cleaning. I was supposed to help and learn. Dad did the grocery shopping. Yikes! He often bought things we didn't want or use and forgot essentials like milk, bread, and cereal. He ended up making many more trips to the grocery store than Mom ever did. Dad wasn't a cook. I give him credit, he tried hard, and he sometimes succeeded in turning out a pretty good dinner. Other times, dinner ended up in the can. Nobody complained. Actually, some of his worst dishes ended in teasing and laughter, which he didn't seem to mind. We ate more meals which just needed to be heated up. Being summer, he often fired up the grill. Megan sometimes had dinner on the table when Dad got home from work. Even though Mr. Number had always been the more serious parent, I believe we recognized that he was trying hard in a situation that was new and difficult for all of us.

Dad enrolled me in several summer camps at the YMCA. There were quite a few classmates as well as kids from other schools at the camps. Missy, a second grader from a different school, was in both of my YMCA sessions. We became good friends. I learned that her parents had divorced before she started school. She lived with her mother and fourth grade sister. Missy saw her dad one evening a week and every other weekend. Even though my parents weren't divorced, I was curious how divorce was for her.

Divorce and all the changes weren't great, and sometimes it was terrible. Missy never got used to it. Sometimes she missed her dad, but quickly stated that she wouldn't want to live with him. She described him as having a temper. He was often busy with work things, even when she and her sister went to visit. Missy also talked about how her mom found a boyfriend several months ago. She did not like the guy. He was at their house way too much, and she complained that her mother acted differently when he was there. She asked how my parents lived in different cities yet weren't divorced. I really didn't have an answer. I said something like, "Mom only moved out a few weeks ago." Missy responded, "Oh, so they will probably get divorced soon." I didn't say anything. I tried to act like it was no big deal, but it really was a big deal. It was always on my mind. I think I just was afraid to admit it to somebody else.

Mom

When Mom first moved out, she called every night, talking to each kid, asking the same questions. After a week or so, the calls got shorter and shorter. Their first big production was coming up at the end of the summer so she would be calling a little less. Believe me, I missed her, but the daily phone calls seemed forced. Don't know about Megan, but I was happy when we spoke only about once during the week and once on weekends.

After about a month, Mom came home for a weekend, arriving Saturday a little after lunch. We were all excited to see her. Dad didn't say much of anything. We hung around the house all afternoon catching up. It was a lot easier than the phone calls. Sometimes it seemed like Gail didn't recognized Mom. She got very excited when talking about her new job. She loved the people she worked with but missed many of her old friends from South Creek. Late afternoon rolled around and we headed out to dinner. Dad, who had left when she arrived, did not come with us. After dinner we hung out at a park for several hours. When it got dark, she drove us home, saying that she had planned to spend the night with her friend Laura but would be back over to see us the next morning. Dad was home when we got back. They spoke briefly in the driveway before she headed off to Laura's. There was no yelling or arguing. They just talked. The day was fun, but strange. There was something different about Mom. I can't really say what it was – just different. What had happened to her in the month since she moved?

Mom came over a little before lunch on Sunday. Dad helped her move some stuff to her car to take to her place. They were polite with each other. We all went out for pizza. Again, everyone seemed to get along. Were they happy to see each other or were they putting on an act in front of us? Who knows? Dad drove so that Mom could leave straight from lunch to go home. He gave her a small hug goodbye as she got in her car. A few tears were shed as Mom drove off. Neither Mom nor Dad said anything nasty all weekend. That was a relief!

Later that night I wondered what was going on. Mom and Dad didn't fight anymore. Why did Dad hug her when she left? Was there any chance that they might get back together someday? Could we possibly all move to her new city? If not, was Missy's prediction of divorce correct? I became upset with myself when I asked if I wanted them to get back together. Of course, I did. How could I have such a thought? Yet, since Mom's announcement that she took the new job, our house, although different, was more peaceful. Peaceful was good, but why couldn't it have been more peaceful when they were together?

The Remaining Summer Days

Looking back, I have to say that the first summer was just strange. Dad was changing, but in a good way. He seemed to get a little less upset when one of us screwed up and even laughed at himself when things didn't go according to plan. We settled into our household jobs and routines, picking up things that Mom had usually done. I didn't miss all the arguing and fighting between them, but it just never seemed right with Mom not around. Missy and I talked a lot about our families. They were different, but they were the same. Each of us were missing one parent in our house. I wanted to ask Dad what happened between them, but I just couldn't. Neither of them had ever sat down with us to talk about what had happened. Megan's eyes got all watery one night when she admitted that she had spent many hours in bed wondering the same things. We made a secret pact to tell each other if we ever found out anything.

Mom continued to call about twice a week, and we shared stuff without her asking fifty questions. Our grandparents took us for a mid-week visit prior to starting school. Mom was really busy but was thrilled to take us to her first theater production at Monroe. It was really cool to think that she designed all the costumes for the show. Mom looked proud as she introduced "my kids" to her fellow theater workers. She had come in several more times that summer, always staying with a friend. Mom and Dad continued to be polite, parting with a hug; however, my hope that they might someday get back together slowly began to fade. I had to work to keep those thoughts out of my head. They made me sad.

School Started

About three weeks into second grade, we had "meet the teacher" night. As we sat in Ms. Bolger's class, I quickly noticed that most kids had both parents present. The next day, Sally, a classmate, asked where Mom had been. I simply told her that she was out of town working. It wasn't a lie, but it certainly wasn't the whole story. I don't recall if I was too embarrassed to tell the total truth, or fearful that she might tell everyone. At recess Ms. Bolger said she was disappointed that Mom had not been able to make it the previous night.

Again, I said that Mom was busy with work, telling her Mom was a costume designer at the theater. Ms. Bolger had been to South Creek Theater several times, stating it must be cool to have a mom involved with professional theater. I enthusiastically said it was; however, I didn't tell her Mom worked in a different theater several hours away. That was the second time I had not been entirely honest about my family. I went home that afternoon not feeling very good about what I had told Sally and Ms. Bolger. For right now, my parents not being together was going to be my secret.

Megan picked up on my funny mood right away. I told her what had happened at school. She admitted that she had only told her two closest friends about Mom moving out of town. I told her about Missy from summer camp. We agreed it felt good to have somebody to talk to. We shared our fears about where this mom and dad thing was headed. Megan again brought up divorce. I didn't understand much about divorce. She tried her best to explain divorce to me, but it was confusing. It frightened me. It sounded so ... final. I guess I had kept alive the wish that either Mom would come back home and get a job back at South Creek, or we would move to her new city and Dad would find a job there. Megan shared that same dream, but I think that's all she thought it was, a dream.

Crisis Number One

The first major family crisis occurred in late October. Megan, being a freshman, became very involved in school activities. Every Friday night she went with her friends to the high school football game. One Friday night it got to be 11:30, and she still wasn't home. Her curfew was 11:00, however, if she called, Dad usually let her stay out a bit longer. No call from Megan this week. I could see Dad getting more and more concerned. Maybe concerned wasn't strong enough. Dad was getting angry. By 11:40 he called the parents of several of Megan's friends. Those girls had been home for some time. By now he was also worried about Megan. I think he forgot that I was still up. Around midnight a car pulled into the driveway. You could hear several different voices laughing. Dad suddenly realized that he had a spectator watching his every move. He pointed to my bedroom. I stood behind the bedroom door listening. Megan immediately apologized for not calling, claiming that she had lost track of time. Dad calmly asked where she had been and with whom. Megan lied. She claimed she had been with the two girls whose parents Dad had just called. Dad blew! I don't know if I had ever heard him get so loud so quick. The yelling must have gone on for ten minutes. I quietly snuck under my covers.

The next morning was more than a little uncomfortable. Dad said good morning but did not look directly at me the entire time we were at the breakfast table. He had to know I heard him screaming at Megan. She had yet to come down by the time I finished eating. Later that morning, I overheard Dad talking to Mom on the phone. He was really upset with Megan but knew he had blown it and was embarrassed. At one point I heard him say something about how he often felt lost trying to raise three girls by himself. Everybody tried to avoid each other the rest of the day. Megan spent most of the day in her room. The next morning Mom was sitting in the kitchen when we got up.

Mom wasn't exactly her usual happy self. She and Dad took Megan out for the "big dating and honesty talk." Megan looked really down when they arrived home. Mom and Dad spent a long time sitting at the picnic table in the back yard talking. They weren't arguing, just talking. He looked really worn out. After lunch Mom, Gail and I went to Megan's soccer game. Part way through the game, I grabbed Mom's hand. She looked at me with both happy and sad eyes. I know, how can you look happy and sad at the same time, but she did. Or maybe that was how I was feeling. On the way home we all stopped for a treat. As we sat eating, Mom asked us how things were around the house. She specifically asked how Dad was doing being the only parent. We didn't lie. We both thought Dad was doing pretty good. We even talked about how he was smiling more and was a little less strict about rules. I believed Gail's presence often brought laughter to the house. Riding home, I wondered whether she got the same story from Dad while sitting at the picnic table. Was he having a harder time than he let on? She headed back shortly after dropping us off.

Crisis Number Two

Crisis number two came several months later. It was Megan again. Freshmen weren't allowed to go to the school Valentine Dance unless they were invited by someone older. Megan was asked by Zeke, a senior. From what I recall from their argument, Dad had several issues. First, Zeke was a senior, way too old in his eyes. Second, Megan only informed him of the dance and her date two days before the big night. Third, they had been seeing each other for over a month and nobody in the family knew. The argument got out of hand quickly. Megan even threatened to go to a friend's house after school Friday and leave for the dance from there. Finally, she screamed, "If Mom was here, she'd let me go. You just don't understand anything about me. I wish I lived with Mom." The line had been crossed. Much to my surprise, Dad quickly cooled as he calmly told her that she wasn't going to the dance. If she wanted to move, he'd help her pack and would call Mom to pick her up this weekend. Dad turned and left the room. Megan was in tears. I don't know if the tears were out of anger or sadness. I was holding Gail while witnessing the whole event. Megan stormed out of the house, not to return for several hours. Nobody said anything to her when she got home.

Dad was there for breakfast the next morning. He was cool with everyone, especially Megan. I expected another blow up. She didn't know how to react. Who was this calm guy? This was not the old dad. Friday night came and Megan was home. Dad told her that she could have several of her girlfriends over if she wanted. She declined. Later that evening Dad went into her room closing the door. It was quiet, no yelling, no anything. He came out about a half hour later and offered to make popcorn. The aroma of popcorn must have been too much for Megan to resist. The three us watched a DVD. Crisis over. Gail slept in peace.

Crisis two brought up some questions I'd never thought of before. Why were we living with Dad? I mean he's a guy and we're all girls. Mom moved in May and appeared settled by the beginning of the school year. Did she not want us? Was her job more important than her daughters? Did Dad fight to keep us? How was the decision made about where the kids would live? I'm not complaining, I missed Mom, but things were going okay with Dad. However, they just never asked our opinion about where to live. And what if I wanted to switch where I lived? Megan expressed her wish to live with Mom. Was it that simple, a phone call, some packing and a four-hour drive?

Where's Mom?

In early March our school had "Mom-Daughter Day." The boys actually stayed home. (There was a Dad-Son Day later in the month.) If we didn't have a mom available, we were allowed to bring a substitute, like a grandma, aunt or even a big sister, as long as they were an adult. There were all sorts of activities for moms and daughters. Mom came with Megan and me last year and it had been the best day ever at school. Megan contacted Mom right after Christmas to see if she was going to be able to make it. Initially, Mom said yes, however a week before the big day she called to tell us that that there was an important event at Monroe Theater, and she had to cancel. She promised to make it up to me with something special in the future. What a downer! We had no relatives in our town so there was no one to substitute for her. Ms. Bolger approached me asking why I had not turned in the Mom-Daughter Reservation Form. I began to cry. We spoke while my classmates went out for recess. I told her what had happened over the last year at my house. She had no idea. Ms. Bolger volunteered to be my substitute mom for the day, indicating that I could also be her helper. Dad was thankful for Ms. Bolger's help while recognizing Megan's anger with Mom for letting me down. Mom was greeted with little enthusiasm on her next visit.

Megan had a minor role in the Freshman Spring Play at school. There was a Friday and Saturday night performance which Mom knew about for weeks. You guessed it, she had a conflict with work. Mom wasn't exactly scoring points with her daughters.

Now What?

We continued to see Mom at home or at her place every several weeks. While visiting in September, she told us we were having dinner with Ben, a friend from the Monroe. This was a surprise. Mom never had any guy friends in the past. Ben was nice, almost too nice, like he was trying to impress us. Megan thought that he was Mom's boyfriend. I didn't understand, Mom and Dad were still married. Were you allowed to do that?

Megan's "boyfriend" idea turned out to be true. By January Mom asked Dad for a divorce. Megan expected it. I feared it. I was shocked. I mean, I didn't love the way things were since she moved out, but I secretly held to the hope that we would get back to the way we were. I never understood this idea that Mom needed her career. What did she mean when she talked about self-fulfillment? Sure, I recognized that she was happy, and I was proud of her work on plays, but wasn't she happy when she was home all the time taking care of us kids?

We were kept pretty much in the dark during the entire divorce process. They both sat us down and told us that we would continue to live with Dad and visits with Mom would be about the same as they had been. None of us uttered a peep until they asked if we had any questions. I asked, "Why divorce?" Before they could answer, Megan sarcastically piped in, "Mom has a boyfriend." We all stared at Mom. She and Ben had become close over the last year or so, and it was just time to make things final. "Are you going to marry Ben?" I asked. Mom didn't directly respond but said that she would never stop loving us. The house was kind of quiet after she left. I guess my hope of a reunion was just a fantasy. I did not sleep well that night. My brain was like a non-stop video of family memories. I felt bad for Dad. He had all the work caring for us. There were no grandparents or aunts or uncles in town to help. It was all on him. Gail, as cute as she was, was growing and getting into everything. More challenges for all of us.

Visits

Remember when they said visits were going to be pretty much the same? Well, they weren't. Mom came to town less and less over the upcoming months. Ben was around a lot when we were there. By our fourth visit, he had moved in. How did that happen? They weren't married! Mom gave us no warning. He was just there when we walked in the door. Ben had been okay in the past, but I wasn't crazy about him being around all the time. We were there to visit Mom, not Mom and Ben. Megan and I whispered to each other that night in the second bed-room. She was not surprised about Ben living there. I thought it was gross that they were sharing a bed. I just wanted to go home. Gail was lucky. She had a cold and stayed with Dad that weekend.

Ben usually did not come to Dad's with Mom, but when he did, he usually stayed in the car. Megan's schedule had become very busy so she didn't always come on outings. I hated when she wasn't there. At least Gail served as a kind of distraction. What was I supposed to do with Mom and Ben? It was much better if just Mom visited. I noticed that Mom and Dad spoke much less since the divorce and there were no goodbye hugs anymore. It was weird. I hated it. Sometimes I wondered if Dad had held out hope that they might get back together. As time passed, I began to worry about him. Mom loved her job and had her boyfriend. Dad had three daughters, who kept him running in circles. He looked tired a lot. Poor dad!

Surprise, Surprise, Surprise!

That Christmas Mom told us that she and Ben were getting married. This was a big surprise to me. Not so much for Megan. The wedding was a small affair held at the Monroe with family, new theater friends and several old friends from our town. Mom wanted a role in the wedding for her daughters. Not to be rude, but neither Megan nor I were excited about her wedding. All three of us stood next to Mom during the ceremony. A wedding day is supposed to be a happy day. Happy was not the way I'd describe how I was feeling. It was awkward! I just wanted it to be over. I just wanted to go home. Gail, of course, was clueless.

That night we stayed in a hotel with our grandparents. Grandma noticed our down mood. We chatted. A big part of the conversation centered around why Mom and Dad ever split up in the first place. Our grandparents said they didn't have a clue. They had no ill feelings toward Dad, and I got the impression over the last year that they judged their daughter as being the big problem in our parent's marriage. They listened as we expressed our feelings, or maybe I should say lack of good feelings about Ben. We didn't hate Ben. We just didn't like him very much. Conversation also centered on how hard Dad worked at being both mom and dad. Even Megan, who recently had run-ins with Dad, expressed how much she worried about him.

Things began to change in the months following the wedding. Mom and Ben moved into a house which gave them much more space. They came to town less often and we visited less. On our visits Mom was more interested in what Ben wanted to do than what we wanted to do. Ben occasionally tried to order us kids around. I didn't get it. He wasn't our dad. What bothered me most was that Mom usually took his side. I began to resent the whole situation more and more. Megan resisted big time. Returning from one visit, Megan stormed into our house informing Dad that she was done visiting "Mom and that man!" Her ranting sparked a thought. Could we not visit Mom if we didn't want to? I began to question my love for Mom. Were my feelings changing for her, or did I just not like having Ben around? I was getting into more arguments with her over little things. I found myself more and more upset after each visit. I felt betrayed.

Fast Forward

The next several years had their share of ups and downs. Over time I became less anxious, or maybe I was less embarrassed about telling school friends or teammates that my parents were divorced. I soon realized that I was not the only one from a split-up family. However, I was the only one I knew who lived with their dad, rarely seeing their mom because she lived so far away. I gradually got more used to not having her around for activities like the mother-daughter soccer game at the end of the season. I was lucky to be included with my friends' families on many occasions.

There were some tough times though, when I really wished I had a mom around. I don't know what it was like for you, but sixth grade was the pits. I know, it's generally a girl thing. You've seen it, us girls all turn into vultures. One girl is your best friend on Monday morning and can't stand you by Tuesday. We blame one another while everyone lies. Tears turn on and off like a water faucet. Insecurity reigns as queen. I just wished Mom had been around. Maybe it was just my fantasy that Mom's presence would have made life easier, more understandable. Who knows, maybe I would have fought with Mom like I did with everyone else.

I started my period the summer between sixth and seventh grades. I knew a little of what to expect from talking with girlfriends. Oh, I can't even think of a word to describe the whole experience. Megan taught me the mechanics, but I wanted something else. She had the "baby talk" with Mom when starting her cycle. Megan talked with me, but neither of us were comfortable. I wanted to call Mom, but it wasn't the conversation to have over the phone. We eventually spoke around two months after things started, but it was just too little, too late. If my parents had only remained together, I think this whole experience might have been easier.

Megan had been my best friend through their split up and divorce. She was around less and became more involved in her own interests as she moved through high school and beyond. She moved out when she started college. I don't hold that against her at all. Sometimes I just really miss not having Megan around more. Luckily, she always answers my texts and every once in a while, she just calls to talk. Occasionally she stops over unannounced and we go out for sister time. Not only was Megan my rock, but she played a big role in keeping the household going after Mom moved out. Some days I think I miss her more than I miss Mom. As I grew, I started taking on more home responsibilities. Dad and I figured it out.

Gail grew into her own little person. She never really knew Mom, so her feelings about the divorce differed from Megan and me. Gail might have been an "Oops Baby," but having a little one around during those early years gave us something positive on which to focus. Even though we might not have realized it at the time, Gail was like that line from a song Dad tried to sing … "sunshine on a cloudy day."

I don't know what to say about Dad. He wasn't the Mr. Number I remember from years ago. Megan, Gail, and I were his girls. Dad still liked things orderly and predictable, but I think he knew he had to change if he was going to keep his family together. He took his oldest daughters shopping for prom dresses, put up with our loud music and outlandish outfits, and learned to accept boyfriends, even though I have to admit that a few of them were … well let's not go there. He learned to laugh at himself, seeming to enjoy life more as he aged. Dad never talked badly about Mom and was always polite when he spoke with her.

I still wonder what went wrong with mom and dad. Granted, I was young when their problems started, but I recall family life as being good. I always wanted to ask them, but I never have. Maybe I don't want to know. Maybe there was some big dark ugly secret which might turn me against one or both of them. Maybe I should just live like the song… "let it be."

Natalie

My name is Natalie. I'm writing this because, well, I'm a mess and my therapist thinks it's a good idea to get my story out. I don't know about that. I'm not even sure about this whole therapy thing. Like, she isn't my first counselor who was going to "save me." Hell, can you save someone whose life is full of nut jobs? I just don't know.

It's the start of eleventh grade. I began the "alternative school track" at my public high school in tenth grade. I've been in what they call Special Ed since third grade. I'm not so sure what's so special about it. The other "speds" were just as stupid as me. All of us sucked at reading and writing, and you also can add math to the list for me. You're probably thinking that if you suck at writing, how can you write a story. I told my story to my therapist who recorded it. She organized it, using my words whenever possible.

Family

I lived with my mom, dad and two older brothers. Jason is seven years older and Duke is six years older. We lived in a trailer park located in the middle of what Jason called "no-where." My dad said rent was cheap and we were away from them "ass-kissing city folks." No parks, stores, movie theaters, swimming pools, not much of anything nearby, just a small town about a fifteen-minute car ride away.

Dad stayed home most days. Sometimes, he'd head out saying he was going to work, but I don't recall that being very often. I have no idea what kind of work he supposedly headed off to. Mom was pretty much the same. Occasionally, she claimed to have a job, but again, I really don't know for sure. We had an old car which always seemed to be broken down. Some days I think I saw Dad's legs hanging out from under the car more than I saw his face. Looking back, maybe that was a good thing.

Now that I'm older, I realize we lived on welfare. Mom had these special things she gave to the checkout person at the grocery store. I asked her once why she didn't pay the checkout lady real money. She yelled at me when we got in the car, telling me to "Mind my own damn business!" This made no sense to me at all. You paid for things with money, didn't you? If we got sick, there was a clinic around a half hour away. I hated going to the clinic. You had to sit in the waiting room forever. I don't ever recall her paying anything at the clinic either.

Trailer Park Paradise

In first grade we had to draw a picture of our house, telling about where we lived. I drew our trailer and described the trailer park. The next day, a classmate said she had asked her mom about a trailer park. Her mom had called us "trailer trash." She asked me what her mom meant by that. I had no idea. I asked my teacher, who just smiled, saying "It means nothing, just forget about it." As an eleventh grader, I get it. If you googled "trailer trash," you'd probably see a picture of my family.

Partying was a full-time occupation for my parents. In spring, summer and fall, they had big bonfires. In the winter, they crammed way too many people into someone's small trailer. Drinking wasn't a party refreshment. It was a nutritional necessity. The music was loud and the nights were late. Looking back, I'm sure alcohol wasn't the only thing the adults were consuming. Once I asked Dad why the adults passed around a cigarette only taking a puff or two. He brushed me off. When I asked Mom, she giggled, giving me some line about how Jesus taught us to share. We never went to church. Where did this Jesus thing come from?

Cheers

In the fall of fifth grade year, I had my first taste of alcohol. It was another typical Saturday night, and you could say most of the adults were well lubricated. I entered our trailer to find Braden, a friend of my parents, getting some beer out of the fridge. He asked if I'd like one. I didn't know what to say. I'd never tasted beer before. He handed me an open can and told me to take a sip. It tasted awful. How could my parents drink that shit? Braden encouraged me to drink more. Yuck, but he kept pushing me. It never really got better, but the more I drank, the less bad it tasted. He eventually went back outside. I poured around half the can down the drain and went to my room, worried what my parent's might do if they found out.

My first beer was on my mind. I was sure it was wrong, but I didn't know what to do about it. I finally told my best friend Ava what had happened. Ava was in the sixth grade, and in my eyes, she knew about everything. Ava laughed, telling me how her dad started giving her sips of beer when she was in the first grade. She and her older sister started sneaking beers from their parents about a year ago. I wanted to know what she thought about the terrible taste. Again, she laughed, saying who cared about the taste. If you drank enough, it made you feel good. Hmmm, maybe that's why my parents were constantly drinking beer. They just wanted to feel good. So why didn't my parents share their beer with me? Ava's dad gave her sips of beer. Were my parents being selfish? Didn't they want me to "feel good?"

Several weeks later, Ava asked me to meet her behind her trailer one Saturday night around 8:30. It was late fall, so it was already dark. The weekend party was well under way down the street. Ava had three beers and wanted to know if I wanted to drink them with her. Part of me said no, but another part said why not, you'll just feel good. Hell, Ava had said so. Over the next hour or so, I drank a little over a beer. It tasted terrible. Ava said I'd get used to it. I can't really say it made me feel good. When I got home that night, I really had to pee. That night in bed, I still wondered what beer was all about.

Ava snuck beers several times a month. It's not like we drank every chance we had, but then she asked if I could steal some beer from my trailer. I hesitated at first, but soon realized how easy it was, so I took a few. We were best friends.

Dad!!

I was coming home from Ava's one Saturday afternoon early in my sixth-grade year when I heard some noise coming from behind a storage building owned by the trailer park. I rounded the corner to see my dad and Lucy, a friend of my parents, playing kissie face. Dad was squeezing her butt and her shirt was unbuttoned. I froze in my tracks. Eventually, they noticed me and quickly separated. I ran!

Dad didn't look at me when he returned for dinner. What was I supposed to do or say? "Mom, you'd never guess what I saw Dad doing today!" "Hey, Dad, is Lucy a good kisser?" "Does Lucy kiss as good as Mom?" Why was Lucy's shirt unbuttoned? What would Mom do if she found out? I quickly ate dinner and headed to Ava's.

I considered telling my brothers but feared how they might handle it. I wanted to tell my best friend Ava, but I was afraid.

Could Ava keep my secret? I feared the whole trailer park would know if I told anyone. Everyone would be looking at me. How would Mom react when she found out? Would Mom be mad at me for not telling her? Mom's a big strong woman. Dad's kind of a scrawny runt. It could get ugly.

As it turned out, I didn't have to say anything. One of Mom's friends saw the whole thing with Lucy. She told Mom that evening when I was at Ava's. As I got back to our trailer, I noticed Jason and Duke sitting outside. There was a war going on inside. Eventually the door slammed open with Dad stomping out screaming every curse word in the book. He eyed me and growled. Oh boy, did he think I told Mom? She eventually came out, looked at us, saying she was going over to her friend Maria's trailer.

We eventually went inside and started cleaning up the mess left from the fight. None of us said a word. Dad didn't come home that night. Mom returned after we had gone to bed. I was still awake. I'd never heard my parents so out of control. I knew what Dad did was wrong, but what was going to happen next? Dad returned late Sunday morning. Jason and Duke were already gone. I headed to my room. I could hear Mom and Dad talking. (There is no privacy in a trailer) There were tears, apologies, and promises. When I left for Ava's, Mom was fixing him a grilled cheese. Problem solved?

Some Never Learn

The next several months seemed to go okay. The name Lucy was never spoken. I have no idea whether she showed up at the weekend adult parties or not. Life with Mom and Dad returned to normal, whatever that means. My best friend Ava and I were always together, sharing beer when we had some.

I guess the temptation of Lucy was too great for Dad. The rumor is that one afternoon in January, Lucy's suspicious live-in boyfriend followed her on what was supposed to be a shopping trip. Lucy's shopping trip ended at the Regal Motel where Dad awaited her arrival. The boyfriend called Mom, who borrowed a neighbor's car, and headed to the Regal. Dad never moved back into the trailer.

Bye, Bye Love ... or Not

Sometime over the next several months they got a divorce. Mom was more than a little bit mad. Her lady friends were around the trailer more than usual. They called Dad a "snake in the grass." Mom said that he was so tiny, he was a redworm in the grass. The ladies howled at this. Redworm became their nickname for Dad. I didn't get it. From what I overheard, Lucy was not his first affair. No forgiveness this time around.

It was different with Dad gone. There had always been lots of yelling, cursing, and name calling, but I never considered it unusual. From my experience, swearing and name calling were part of our family. There was a period of several months when Mom seemed lost. She moped around and occasionally jumped us. She started drinking beer with lunch, continuing through the rest of the day. She became more lax with chores, and my brothers usually did the grocery shopping.

I never considered myself particularly close to Dad, but I wished he was home. Did I miss him, or did I miss the way things had been? Our family wasn't exactly the perfect TV family, but ideal or not, it was my family. He stopped by several times with one of his buddies to get his stuff. I had no idea where he was living. He said we'd do something "fun" as soon as he got settled. I didn't see him until summer when he stopped over to take Jason and Duke fishing. Where was my "fun time" with Dad?

Mom wasn't herself and Dad was gone. I felt parentless. I felt anger and resentment. I was still in grade school. I needed parents. Jason and Duke were adults. Jason was a year out of high school and was looking for full-time work. I suspected he would be moving out when he found it. Duke just graduated, had a girlfriend, and was rarely home. I felt alone in our trailer.

Summertime

Summertime in a rural trailer park meant boring time. We girls had to create our own fun. As long as we stayed out of the adults' way, they were happy. We continued to sneak beer and Ava introduced me to cigarettes. I had been around smokers all my life, but I coughed on my first several puffs.

Ava thought smoking was cool, so I thought it was cool too. We thought we were the badass drinking, smoking trailer park girls.

One afternoon Ava suggested we walk into town. A fifteen-minute car ride was like an hour and a half walk. We were tired, thirsty and penniless. Great planning, don't ya think? After walking around for a while, she told me to sit on a bench outside the grocery store while she went inside. I began to wonder what was taking her so long. A store worker came out looking for me. Ava was sitting in a small office having been caught shoplifting two sodas. The police arrived and took us home. I was terrified! I guess we weren't so badass after all.

I hadn't actually shoplifted, but Mom still lost it. I was with Ava who got caught and the police were at our trailer. The whole trailer park would soon know of our little adventure. Yelling, screaming, cussing, threatening, you name it. Just so happened my brothers were both home. They thought the whole situation was a hoot. Their little sis had finally grown up. She had her first run-in with the police. Their laughing and teasing only made Mom madder. It was late afternoon and she had probably drunk more than a few beers, which probably made things worse. I got extra chores and was grounded to the trailer for two weeks. I was out in two days. I don't think Mom could stand having me around.

Turn The Page

Mom finally came out of her funk around the end of summer. She started going to weekend adult parties and took more interest in her appearance and the overall condition of the trailer. My incident in town was in the rearview mirror.

By the end of September, I had an idea why I had seen changes in Mom. Braden, the guy who gave me my first beer, started sniffing around. Braden used to live with some woman and her two kids, but I heard she kicked him out. No idea why, but I heard talk about him having difficulty keeping his zipper up. Gross!

Trailer parks are basically one giant rumor mill. Everybody was into everybody else's business. Who's sleeping with whom, who's fighting, was anybody in trouble with the police, divorce on the horizon, unwanted pregnancies. You name it, everybody knew it. Ava heard her mom on the phone talking about my mom and Braden sleeping together. Eww eww eww! Braden was an ugly jerk. The thought of him kissing my mom turned my stomach. The thought of him in my mom's bedroom ... I can't go there! My dad was a skinny little guy, but Braden was a fat beast. He started coming over more and more in the evening. I was scared where this Mom and Braden thing was headed. My brothers were rarely around, so it was basically me, Mom and him. The more he hung around, the more he started to make himself at home. He ate our food and drank Mom's beer. He never brought anything but his disgusting self. If I sat on the couch, he plopped down next to me. He gave me the creeps. He'd order me to get him beers and he picked what was on TV. Sometimes, he watched movies which I'm positive were not for seventh graders.

Eventually I had to talk to Mom. Well, it was useless. Mom was all about Braden. She defended everything he did. She had no problem with him ordering me around. Hell, I was just a kid. Mom said he was a good man with a nice car and good paying full-time job. Hmm .... is that what this was all about? Was Braden the answer to her money problems? I don't recall Dad ever having a full-time job. By Thanksgiving, he was almost a fixture, but by Christmas he became a permanent one.

Help!!!!

Wintertime sucks in a trailer park. It's dark early and cold outside. There's no privacy in the paper-thin walled trailers. Sometimes I'd wake at night hearing noises coming from Mom's bedroom. YUCK! I tried to spend as much time as possible at Ava's, but her mother often asked about Mom and Braden, whom she referred to as "middle aged love birds." There was no getting away from it. By now Jason had found a job and had moved out of the park with a friend. Duke spent most nights at his girlfriend's place.

We continued to steal beer whenever possible. Two and a half bottles a piece became our goal. The effects of more beer became noticeable. I liked it. Ava and I became more daring. I had grown to like the little buzz from cigarettes which were easy to steal. By spring, two ninth graders from the park,

Owen and Jerry joined us. They brought more beer and cigarettes which was great They were only two years older than me. I was pretty clueless about boys. My education was about to begin. Anything had to be better than being at home with Mom and Braden.

School

As I said earlier, I'm not much of a student. They said I was "learning disabled," whatever that is. At first, Special Ed was good, a lot less pressure, and I started to feel better about myself. My teacher, Mrs. Cranley, was cool. She used different ways to teach me how to read. However, my improving self-concept began to fade in sixth grade. Even though I had become a better reader, I stilled sucked compared to my peers. Textbooks, especially in science and social studies, were much too difficult. I hated having my teachers read tests for me and change assignments so I could handle them. By the end of sixth grade I began to see myself for what I really was, a dumb kid from the trailer park.

I'd never been in any kind of big trouble prior to seventh grade. Well, that was about to change. I didn't see Ava much at school since she was in eighth grade. I started hanging with three other kids at school. Two lived in a different trailer park and one was a townie, so I rarely saw them outside of school. The first incident occurred the day before Halloween. One kid brought in rolls of black and orange toilet paper. (Don't ask where she got it.) We hung around after school and toilet-papered two girls' restrooms. I thought it was an improvement, you know, to add a little color. The principal wasn't amused. One day of in-school suspension was our punishment. Mom was pissed! No going out for Halloween and two weekends grounded. I didn't care. I was too old to go out anyways. Braden got involved. Who did he think he was? He wanted to take a belt to me, but Mom stopped him.

The next major crime came the night of the Christmas choral concert which involved all seventh graders. Our little posse thought it would be fun to put chewing gum on the risers. Again, the principal did not share our humor. We got a three-day suspension. Mom went ballistic. More groundings, which were never fully carried out. I was required to see the school counselor upon returning to school. This lady was so old that the kids referred to her as "Granny" behind her back. Those meetings were useless. She thought she could get in my head. Idiot!

School just went downhill from there. There was another suspension in the spring for bringing a water gun filled with red juice to school. I'd had it with several preppy girls who thought their shit didn't stink! I never did homework anymore. There were more parent conferences. At one point, I wasn't sure if Mom was madder at me, or the principal and teachers for constantly calling her. Thank God for summer!

Boys…A One-Track Mind

Ava, Owen, Jerry, and I were always together during the summer before eighth grade. Owen and Ava became kind of sweet on each other. They'd sometimes head off to be alone which left me with Jerry. That was awkward. Jerry was nice and all, but I really wasn't looking for a boyfriend. I tried to talk to Ava about it, but she told me, "Relax, boys can be fun." She giggled when she said it. I'm not stupid. I knew what she and Owen were doing, or at least I thought I did.

It didn't take long for me to figure out what Jerry was interested in. One warm, humid night in July, the four of us had been drinking at an isolated pond we hung out at which was outside the trailer park. Ava stood up announcing that it was hot so she was going skinny dipping. The boys quickly followed. I wasn't so sure. Their taunting and teasing increased. Eventually I caved and joined them. Ava and Owen were all over each other. I gradually relaxed. Jerry came up behind me from under water and kissed the back of my neck. I quickly turned and he planted one on me. It was my first real kiss and here I was, skinny dipping with a boy two years older than me. We were basically two couples for the rest of the summer. Jerry was swinging for a home run. I was happy with a double.

Caught!

I can remember clear as day the first time I got caught after drinking too much. Braden was the only one home when I stumbled into the trailer. He recognized my tipsy condition. He started into me. At times he sounded angry, whereas at other times he seemed to be making fun of me. All I wanted to do was go to bed. He demanded that I stay up with him until Mom got home. Braden slapped the couch next to him telling me to have a seat. I nervously sat waiting for Mom. The guy is creepy. He kept looking at me with this weird smile. He wanted to know if Jerry was my boyfriend. He asked what we did when we were out together. I now recognize he was feeding his sexual perversions.

I was relieved when Mom opened the door; however, Braden, who had just started to back off, shifted into overdrive. He provided an exaggerated version of my condition and what he believed was going on between Jerry and me. He sarcastically laughed as he spewed how his "little girl" was growing into a woman. First of all, I never was, and never will be, his little girl! I guess he thought he was funny when joking about young love and alcohol leading to little babies. Mom listened in silence. I could see the increasing tension on her face. When he finished, Mom pointed to my room. As I glanced back, I noticed she was giving Braden "the eye."

I kept trying to keep from throwing up as Mom entered my room. She let me have it with both barrels. She started on alcohol and went from there. I didn't try to defend my behavior; however, I kept thinking, you drink all the time, what's the big deal? Looking back, I can't believe she hadn't suspected me of drinking in the past. Maybe she was just too drunk herself to notice, or care.

Mom was calmer when she shifted gears to talk about Jerry. I had started my period early in the sixth grade; however, she provided very little information about making babies. Up to that point, I had learned more about boys from Ava than anyone. I swore to Mom that Jerry and I never "did it." I'm not sure she believed me.

I wasn't sure how I felt that night in bed. Ava and I had been sneaking beer for several years. I never thought about consequences after the first several months. I knew drinking was supposed to be an adult thing, but we weren't causing any harm. We weren't getting wasted like many of the adults at the trailer park did every weekend. The whole boyfriend thing was confusing. I had grown to enjoy Jerry's company, but I didn't consider him my boyfriend. Sure, we did a few things, and I had grown to like how it made me feel. Is that wrong? Braden scared me now more than ever. I didn't like the things he said or the way he looked at me. I never felt that way around Dad. I didn't bring that up with Mom.

Eighth Grade

Within days of the new school year, Jerry and Owen, who were now sophomores, moved on with friends from outside the park. Ava, now a freshman, was around much less. By mid-October, I was feeling more abandoned, spending more time on my own.

The only good thing about school was reconnecting with my posse from last year. We continued to test the limits and ended up in the principal's office on a regular basis. They didn't know what to do about us and we really didn't care. In or out of school suspensions were no big deal. By now Mom rarely added on any type of home punishment. She almost acted bored when taking a school phone call or attending a conference. She never argued with school staff; however, she rarely carried through with their suggestions. I remember a meeting when Mom was told that if I didn't change, I'd never graduate high school. No emotional response from Mom. Couldn't she defend me, yell at them, blame me or yell at me, or just try to help me? I wondered if she cared. I was feeling more alone.

Granny, the old school counselor, finally retired. I soon met Ms. Bates, a young, enthusiastic, hyper school counselor. I was hesitant at first. However, I slowly warmed to her. We didn't have regularly scheduled meetings, but we talked several times a month. Ms. Bates never lectured me about my poor grades or school behavior. She didn't play one hundred questions about my family. One day after a big snow, we spent our entire time talking about the fun of snow days. I might not have admitted it then, but I enjoyed seeing Ms. Bates.

Ava changed since starting high school. She dressed differently and seemed to have a new boyfriend every couple of weeks. When I saw her, she usually was with several new high school friends. I never felt comfortable with them. Her friends often laughed at things I did or said, not because I was funny, but because they considered themselves cool, and I wasn't. By Christmas, I rarely saw Ava anymore.

OMG!!!

One evening when Mom wasn't home, I fell asleep on the couch while watching a DVD. I woke to use the bathroom. I opened the door and there stood fat, creepy, naked Braden. Our eyes locked. Braden smiled. I slammed the door and ran to my bedroom. Within minutes, he knocked on my locked door. I didn't respond. He said something like, "haven't you ever seen a naked man before?" He laughed saying, "I bet you've seen Jerry naked many times." "Jerry is just a boy, I'm a man!" I was terrified that he might break into my room. Luckily, I heard the trailer door open, Mom was home. I waited till I heard their bedroom door close to rush to the bathroom. My bladder and head were both ready to explode.

It was really late when I fell asleep. I kept thinking, don't most people lock the bathroom door when showering? I always do. Why did Braden smile and not quickly close the door? What did he think by coming to my room and saying those sick things? Oh God, do you think he was naked outside my door? I'm not stupid, I knew that sometimes young girls were sexually abused by older men. Would that have happened to me if Mom hadn't come home? I tried to push those thoughts out of my mind. I didn't know what to do. Would Mom even believe me if I told her? She almost always stood up for Braden. I liked my posse, but I wasn't close enough to share this horrible night with any of them. Did I really even want to tell anybody? It would be so embarrassing. I wished Ava was still around like old times. What had just happened? I was terrified!

Could It Get Worse?

I couldn't stand Braden before the shower thing. Now I was also scared of him. It was winter, and I was stuck in the trailer a lot. Sometimes, I couldn't avoid being home alone with him. I often caught him staring at me. Creepy, creepy, creepy! He made remarks like "Nat is starting to grow little Nat boobs." "You're going to fill out that bathing suit real nice next summer, aren't you, little Nat?" "If Jerry could see you now, he'd be pounding on our door." It dawned on me that he never made those types of remarks when Mom was around. Several times while watching TV, Braden plopped himself on a chair next to me and put his hand on my knee while talking. I always bolted to my room. He'd laugh, saying something like "Where you going, little Nat? Don't you like talking to Braden?"

I spent more time in my room. I was lonely, scared, and desperately missed Ava. Things weren't great when Dad was around, but a least there was no Braden. What did Mom ever see in him? I know he had steady work, but we still never seemed to have any extra money. I wanted to tell her how he acted when she wasn't home, but I was scared. What could I do to get out of this situation? There was no place to go and no one to go to. God, please don't let them get married!

One Saturday night I was home alone while Mom and Braden were at the weekend party. The door opened and in stumbled Braden. After using the bathroom, he grabbed beer from the fridge and left. Whew! I went to the fridge to get a soda, spotting his cell on the floor. I couldn't resist. They wouldn't be back for hours. I knew his code because he'd told it to Mom many times. One, two, three, four, five, six, he's a genius, don't you think? I was going through texts and photos when suddenly there I was. I couldn't believe my eyes. Braden had pictures of me in various stages of undress from my bedroom and bathroom. I thought I was going to throw up. After a few minutes, I took the phone to my room and hid it. I didn't know what to do. I tried calling Ava, but she didn't answer. I was awake in bed when they got home. I could hear Braden complaining that he'd lost his phone. Mom didn't pay much attention. I'm not sure I slept at all that night. I kept asking myself how he got those pictures of me in my bedroom and bathroom. Did he share those pictures with other pervs? God, if they were on the net, anybody could see me. I was totally freaked!

Despite getting little sleep, I was up first. They came out around 11:00. Braden asked if I had seen his phone. Of course, I said no. He kept looking at me as if he didn't believe me. I quickly grabbed my coat and headed to Ava's. Thank God she had just gotten up. She reluctantly invited me in. After her shower, I told my previous and only best friend what had been going on.

Time for Action

Ava immediately asked to see Braden's phone. Ava, who isn't exactly a saint, couldn't believe her eyes. We knew we had to tell somebody, but who? Neither of us trusted telling any adults from the trailer park. We finally decided on Ms. Bates, my school counselor. Ava volunteered to hold the phone for safe keeping. I was relieved when she asked me to spend the night.

Monday morning arrived and I went straight to Ms. Bates's office. I'd never been so nervous. I had not slept much for several days and was too upset to eat breakfast. She was in a meeting. I refused to go to class, insisting it was an emergency. One of other the counselors offered to help, but I insisted it had to be Ms. Bates.

Ms. Bates seemed happy yet surprised to see me. In the past she had always called me to talk. I stared at the floor as I sat in her office. She patiently waited me out. Within minutes I was a hot mess of tears. She was not pushy with questions. Slowly I began to tell what had been going on at my house. I never felt as if she doubted a word I said. Eventually the phone pictures came up. I told her my friend had the phone at her house.

I did not go to class that day. Ms. Bates got me something to eat and headed off to find the principal. They both returned telling me that they had to contact the authorities. Within an hour Mrs. Klink from a place called Jobs and Family Services arrived. Ms. Bates remained with me as I spoke with Mrs. Klink. They both repeatedly told me that I had done the right thing in coming to Ms. Bates. Officer Stein, from the County Sheriff's Department, arrived around noon. He informed us that he would be visiting Ava at the high school so he could retrieve the phone. They got me lunch, but I really wasn't hungry. I sat and waited in Ms. Bate's office, worried about what was going to happen next.

Around 1:30 Officer Stein and a lady who was introduced as Detective Howard arrived. Again, they praised me for having the courage to see Ms. Bates. They repeatedly told me that I was not responsible for any of this. They were trying to contact Mom. I just sat waiting, not knowing what to do. Even though they told me it wasn't my fault, I wasn't so sure. What was Mom going to do when they told her? Would she believe them? Physical and emotional exhaustion were starting to overwhelm me. Couldn't I just go sleep and make this all go away?

The next several hours dragged on forever. School was out and I was still there. It was like all the adults were walking on eggshells around me. Nobody knew what to say. Thank God for Ms. Bates. We took several walks after the kids had gone home. As it was getting dark around 6:30, Officer Stein returned with my mom. We both stood staring at each other, neither knowing what to say. Eventually I broke down and Mom opened her arms as tears ran down her face. Everything crashed inside of me at once.

Braden was arrested on Child Pornography and other charges. I didn't understand it all, but I really didn't care. He was gone. That evening was tough. We were dead silent on the ride home. Mom apologized over and over again when we got home. She swore up and down that Braden would never enter our trailer again. I didn't know exactly how I felt about her. I get why she divorced Dad but could never understand how she fell for Braden. Sure, she had been unhappy for months, but even I had heard rumors about him from the trailer park. Maybe she never saw the sexual stuff towards me, but how could she not notice all the other crappy ways he treated me. Hell, he treated her like crap, too.

The Few Next Days

I was exhausted, and uneasy about returning to school. Detective Howard visited our trailer Tuesday and spoke to Mom and me separately. She said it was very unlikely that I would ever have to appear in open court. I might have to meet with a prosecutor and judge in a private meeting, but she would be with me. Detective Howard repeatedly reassured me that I would never have to face Braden again. A social worker would be out to visit us soon.

Ava stopped by Tuesday evening. We spent a long time in my room. I wanted to tell her how much I missed our friendship since she went to high school, but I just didn't know how. Ava expressed how she couldn't get those terrible pictures out of her head and was relieved when the police showed up asking her for Braden's phone. For a short spell it seemed like old times, yet I knew we would drift apart again.

On Wednesday I started my school day with Ms. Bates. I feared that all the kids would know what had happened. I could feel their eyes burning into me as I walked down the hall to the school counselor's offices. What would they think, say, or do if they knew a man had taken pictures of me when I was naked? Would they believe that I had no idea the pictures were being taken? Ms. Bates tried to assure me that nobody knew anything. She gave me a pass to her office that I could use anytime I felt overwhelmed.

The rest of the day crawled along. Even though no kids said anything, I feared they knew what had happened and were avoiding me. Even my posse seemed different. I can't really explain how, but they did. I ate lunch in the counseling office area just to avoid everyone. My social studies teacher asked where I had been the last two days. Did he really care or was he just fishing for information? I couldn't wait to get on the bus to go home.

Mrs. Loew, a social worker, was at our trailer when I got home. She worked with young girls who had been victims of sexual abuse. I think I knew that I was sexually abused, yet I had never let the actual words "sexual abuse" settle in my head. Although I'd been scared, mad, and anxious, I had managed to bury those feelings. I had learned about sexual abuse in health class, and I knew something about it from TV and movies, but now here it was, right in front of me. Talking with Mrs. Loew made it real. I felt sick. I was a victim of sexual abuse! More sleepless nights as I relived the last several months over and over again in my head. I had no energy for anything.

Follow Up

I began to meet with Mrs. Loew weekly at school. She was young, nice, and seemed to care, but I had a hard time warming up to her. She asked about Mom and Dad's relationship, their divorce, did I see Dad, about school, boyfriends, and much more. She always wanted to know how I felt about things. Mrs. Loew didn't push the thing with Braden.

The more we met, the more I began to question my life. I sort of knew my family fit the bill of 'trailer trash,' but up until now, it hadn't mattered. My dad was nuts and I didn't see Mom as much better. Were they both alcoholics? Didn't they realize I was basically free to do whatever, while they were off partying? How did they not know I had been drinking since the fifth grade? I understood why my brothers got out the first chance they had. I was becoming more alone and depressed. Why couldn't I have been born to a mom and dad who never got divorced and didn't drink themselves silly every weekend. Why couldn't I have had parents who cared more about their kids than themselves?

I found it harder and harder to go to school each morning. I had become what some kids called a "counseling office groupie." Ms. Bates had become my go-to person. Sometimes I just sat in her office and we said hardly anything. I know she cared, but I also knew she couldn't change my past or how I felt. My grades continued to suck; however, I cared less than before, if that's even possible. I lost interest in the posse within weeks of returning to school. Their crazy pranks and goofing off seemed childish. As I predicted, Ava returned to her high school friends. The school year ended, and I was off to high school. How was I going to live without Ms. Bates? She was the only reason I went to school.

Home

Even though Mom apologized like a million times, she never really understood what I had gone through. Mom accepted that Braden did horrible, bad things, but she couldn't understand why I wasn't able to move on, to get over it. Within several weeks, she had returned to the weekend adult parties at the trailer park. Mom apparently was ready to make him history, happy to wash away any memories in a bath of beer. I began to fear that she might bring home another man.

It was summertime and I was alone with nothing to do. Mrs. Loew visited us at our trailer every other week. She recognized I was in a bad way and convinced Mom to allow her to make an appointment with a specialist. Hell, Mom didn't care as long as it didn't cost her anything. In early August, she took us to see Dr. Kirkland. He spoke with Mom and me separately. I believe Mrs. Loew had filled him in on my situation. Dr. Kirkland prescribed some pills for my depression. He'd see me again in several months.

High School

Freshman year started and I felt more alone than ever. I went to class, but I just couldn't get into it. I didn't think the pills from Dr. Kirkland made much difference. I was too afraid to stop by the counseling office to seek out my assigned counselor. I continued to see Mrs. Loew.

By the end of freshman year, I had earned two credits, which were probably a gift. Basically, I was still a freshman. I didn't get in trouble as I had in my younger years. I just didn't do much more than show up. A meeting was held with the assistant principal, counselor, my special ed teacher, Mrs. Loew, and my mom. They suggested I start tenth grade in the "alternative school," located in a separate building near the football field. They said I would take classes on the computer at my own pace with a teacher present to assist. I think Mom would have agreed to send me to Mars for school. She just wanted to go home.

Alternative school had nineteen students and wasn't all bad. The teacher was cool, and there was no pressure. Mrs. Loew was replaced by Dr. Jamison, a therapist with whom I met twice a month. Throughout sophomore year, my depression and loneliness increased, despite several medication changes by Dr. Kirkland. I had no close friends, spending most of my time at home listening to music in my room. Dr. Jamison questioned whether I thought about hurting myself. I'd be lying if I said the thought never crossed my mind. Mom had found a new boyfriend, but thankfully he had not moved in. I rarely saw my brothers. Occasionally I saw Dad in the trailer park with his old friends, but he pretty much ignored me. I was told that Braden was in prison. Good!

Thoughts

I really don't like being the way I am – so unhappy, so lonely. Sometimes I spend hours fantasizing about a different life. I know most families aren't like what you see on TV, but then again, most parents also aren't nuts like mine either. Sure, we lived in a trailer park with some off-the-wall families, but they aren't all that way. I realized that most parents didn't get blitzed every weekend. Most adults left the park each day to go to work. I'd heard about affairs, but from what I've learned, it was a hobby with my dad. Why was I drinking in the fifth grade? Maybe it was a way to belong? Even though I miss Ava, we did some pretty stupid crap. Mom deserved companionship after Dad, but Braden, come on Mom! The guy had a reputation as a creep around the park before Dad left. I can't stop thinking about what might have happened to me if I hadn't told Ms. Bates. Thinking back, I believe Ms. Bates was maybe the best person I ever had in my life. God, I wished she had moved to the high school with me.

I still don't know how he took those pictures. I have trouble letting myself trust boys from school, even though they have done nothing to deserve such treatment. Yeah, I'm a mess. I'm scared of the future, like what's to become of me. Dr. Jamison thinks telling my story will help. Maybe my first grade classmate's mom was correct when she referred to my family as trailer trash. I don't know, I just don't know.

Emma

My name is Emma and I'm in ninth grade. I live with mom and my two sisters, Maggie, ten, and Simone, seven. Maybe I should call them half sibs. You see, we each have a different daddy. I've been in five schools if you count preschool. Christa, my mom, works in admissions at a retirement community. She's thirty-one. Sounds a little young to have a ninth-grader, don't you think? She was seventeen when I was born.

Getting Started

I remember Mom telling the story about how I popped out on a snowy Monday morning in February during her senior year of high school. She said being pregnant in high school was no big deal. I wonder what she'd say if I got pregnant in a few years! My dad, Clint, was in her grade. They had dated eight months before he knocked her up. Mom said they were "deeply in love." Okay, "deeply in love" at seventeen, maybe, but why a baby? Mom and I had "the baby talk" when I was in sixth grade. Obviously, she had not practiced what she now preaches. We started out living with Grandma. Grandpa died years before I was born. Grandma worked as a seamstress out of her house and was always making wedding dresses and fancy outfits.

Marriage 101

Clint got a job after graduation driving an ice delivery truck. He was over most evenings and weekends helping with different things. He popped the question at Christmas and a spring wedding was planned. By the wedding, I was a little over a year old and was walking everywhere. I've asked Mom about her wedding several times over the years. Mom seemed both happy and sad talking about it. Recently, she pulled out an old, yellowed photo album. I thought she was gorgeous in the knee length white dress Grandma had made special for her. Clint, or should I say Dad, wore a bow tie. He was quite the handsome devil. I was in many of the wedding pictures. I'm not bragging, but I must say, I was awfully cute. The wedding was held at Grandma's church. A party was held in the backyard at my other grandparent's house. From the pictures, it looked like everyone had a great time.

The three of us lived with Grandma. Everyone got along at first. Grandma was thankful for Clint's help with things like yardwork and other household chores. Mom worked breakfast and lunch shifts at the Diner, so Grandma worked her sewing around watching me before Mom returned early afternoon.

My parents tried to save money to get their own place, but I guess saving money was hard. Six months turned into a year with no sign of us leaving Grandma's. Grandma wasn't a neat freak, but Dad became a slob. He wanted cable in their bedroom, but Grandma believed no house needed more than one TV. Although she did most of the cooking, he made requests that she buy certain foods. He helped with house stuff less and less. Daddy believed a baby was "woman's work." He started hanging out more with friends from high school. Mom rarely went out because she had to watch me so Grandma could do her sewing.

Eventually, we got our own apartment. Grandma still helped with babysitting. The workload for Mom increased. Now she did the cooking, shopping and cleaning, whereas before Grandma took on many of those chores. Daddy became less helpful, spending more time in front of the TV or with friends. He joined a softball team with the "boys" from work. They always stayed around after games to party. Money was always an issue. Mom could have picked up extra dinner shifts at the Diner, but rarely did because then she'd have to rely more on Grandma to watch me. Daddy complained if he had to stay with me by himself. After several months in their own place, mom's frustrations grew. Fights increased.

By age two, Mom described me as her little talking tornado. We occasionally got together with Karen from the Diner, her husband Todd, and son Steve. Daddy was rarely there, always claiming to have other plans. Mom told many stories of the good times the five of us had together without Daddy. Mom recalled how they were constantly yelling at each other back then. Being so young, I didn't have any idea what was going on. Even after I was toilet trained, he still complained if he had to stay by himself with me.

One Saturday after my nap, I found Grandma and Mom seated on the couch. Mom had been crying. She didn't look hurt, so what was up? I knew something was not right. Grandma took me out for a treat. Mom and Karen had gone shopping, and she picked me up after dinner. The apartment was empty when we got home, no Daddy.

The Beginning of The End

Daddy wandered in the next morning. The yelling started. I ran to my room crying. Mom came to me shortly after the apartment door slammed. Mom wasn't crying. She just looked, I don't know how to describe it, different, mad, frustrated, relieved, sad, I don't know. Years later Mom told me that this was not the first time Daddy had not come home at night. She had enough! Daddy, her one-time "true love" and father of her child, was not the guy she married. He cared only about himself. He spent more time with friends than he did with family, and he didn't lift a finger to help out. He was around very little over the next several weeks. and he ignored us when he was home. Daddy showed no interest in me.

One Saturday morning I awoke to find Grandma, Karen, and Todd at our apartment. Why was everyone there so early? Mom took me to my room and said that we were moving back to Grandma's. Daddy was staying at the apartment. I really didn't get it. Karen, Todd, and Grandma were there to help us move. The next several hours were a rushed blur. Sometime after lunch we had everything together and were off to Grandma's house. Still no sign of Daddy. Now I realize that maybe it was planned that way.

Back to GM's

Within days of moving back to Grandma's, Mom seemed happier. They never mentioned Daddy's name in front of me. I occasionally asked if he was going to ever stop by and got the response, "I don't know." Maybe what they really wanted to say was, "I hope not."

Then one Sunday several months after our move, Daddy stopped by. Grandma answered the door but did not invite him in. He saw me behind her. I yelled "Hi." He just nodded. I had no idea what to do. I was a little scared. Mom was in the basement doing laundry. I ran to get her. She and Daddy talked on the porch. Grandma took me to the kitchen which was in the rear of the house. A little while later, Mom came back inside. They made eye contact. Mom shook her head and rolled her eyes. She returned to the basement to finish with laundry. She seemed okay when she came back upstairs.

Over the next several months, I stopped asking about Daddy. Nobody seemed to miss him, and Mom was in a much better mood. One evening while getting ready for bed, Mom told me that she and Daddy were never going to live together again. I don't recall asking why, I don't think I cared, it just didn't matter to me. Daddy hadn't been involved in my young life. Mom and Grandma were my life. I didn't need anything else.

Moving On

Mom continued working at the Diner and Grandma was busy as ever with her sewing. I started pre-school three mornings a week in the fall. I was excited to have other kids to play with. Mom started working extra hours on days I attended pre-school. She went out on weekends with girlfriends who were always real nice to Grandma and me. I think Grandma was happy to see Mom have a little fun.

Later that fall, I heard Mom telling Grandma that she'd been seeing a guy named Gerald whom she'd met at a party. Grandma asked Mom if they were serious. What did "serious" mean? I burst around the corner into the kitchen asking who was Gerald? Grandma looked at me, smiling while waving her finger, saying, "Look who's here, Miss Nosey." Mom repeated that Gerald was a friend. I asked Grandma what she meant when she asked Mom if she was serious. Grandma asked, "How long were you standing there listening to us, Miss Nosey?" Everybody had a good laugh. Grandma dodged answering by grabbing the cookie jar off the kitchen counter. Smooth move, Grandma!

The following Saturday Mom was all dressed up, telling Grandma she was going out to a club and would be home late. I asked was she seeing, her new friend Gerald? She smiled. I turned to Grandma who laughed, saying "Miss Nosey, you're at it again!" They both cracked up as Mom's ride arrived. She gave me a big hug before she walked out the door. Mom and Grandma seemed okay, so I was too.

Number Two

Sometime after Christmas something seemed to change with Mom. She became cranky and was always tired. I had no idea what was up. Mom called in sick to work a couple of mornings, and I think I heard her throwing up in the bathroom several days.

One evening, Mom sat down with Grandma and me and announced that she was going to have a baby. I didn't know what to think. Obviously, I had no idea how a baby got inside Mom's belly. Was this a good thing? Was Mom happy? I really couldn't tell. What did Mom expect me to say or do? She didn't have a big belly which made the whole thing harder to believe. Grandma got out of her chair, crossed the room, sat on the couch, and gave her a loving hug. They didn't say anything. When they separated, Mom had tears rolling down her cheeks. Grandma pulled me over as we all sat in silence for several minutes. I wanted to say something, but Miss Nosey was suddenly speechless. We eventually made our way to the kitchen where Grandma made hot chocolate.

The Next Seven

Mom's body changed as her tummy grew larger. She wasn't throwing up anymore and was less cranky. She continued to work at the Diner but was more tired in the evenings. She stopped going out at night with friends. Mom shopped with girlfriends who occasionally hung around our house which left her in a good mood. This baby thing seemed okay. We were all happy.

One evening Mom started giggling as she sat on the couch watching TV. I noticed she was staring at her belly where she had placed her hands. She invited me to sit next to her as she put my hands on her belly. What was this all about? She told me to be still. Out of nowhere, her belly moved. I looked startled as Mom broke into a big smile. "That's the baby." The baby, really? How did she know? I kept my hands there for a long time but nothing else happened. Mom explained that the baby was growing and sometimes wanted to move around and stretch, just like we move around at night when we sleep in our beds. Okay, I guess that made sense. I wanted to know if it hurt when the baby kicked. Mom just grinned. Over the next several months she got bigger and bigger. I got to feel the baby move around and kick almost every day. It was fun!

My Aunt Sally, Uncle Jake, and their son Max were around a lot since Daddy was gone. I don't think they ever liked him. Luckily, most of the baby stuff Mom had for me was still in Grandma's basement. They spent weekends building a sewing room in the basement and painting bedrooms. I loved having them around. There was excitement in the house.

I sometimes wondered about my daddy. Even though I had not seen him in a long time, he still was my daddy. Being four,

I wondered if the new baby had a daddy. Did everybody have to have a daddy? Gerald was the only man Mom had ever mentioned since Clint left. I hadn't heard Gerald's name in forever. I knew one of the girls from pre-school lived with her daddy. There was no mommy around. How could that be? I was confused but didn't ask any questions.

July fifteenth arrived like any other day. It was hot and Grandma had promised to refill our small backyard pool after lunch. By now, Mom was humongous. She looked kind of funny when she tried to get out of a chair. Her boss at the Diner allowed her to spend most of her shift working the register. We were already filling the pool when Mom got home a little earlier than usual. Grandma took one look at her and said go inside, no swimming today. I protested but Grandma was firm.

I didn't know what was going on. I sat in the kitchen while Grandma went into Mom's room. I had a puzzled look as she came out reaching for the phone to call Mom's baby doctor. I still didn't have a clue. Grandma informed me that Karen was coming over shortly. At that point, Mom called me into the room. I'll never forget her words, "You're going to become a big sister real soon!"

The next half hour was full of commotion. Grandma was running around putting clothes in a gym bag for me as Karen arrived. I was constantly in and out of Mom's room. Every several minutes she got these really painful looks on her face. I got scared! Was this supposed to happen when you had a baby? Eventually it was time for me to leave with Karen. As Mom started to hug me goodbye, she stiffened, appearing in pain. What was going on? Grandma and Karen helped Mom to the car as Steve and I watched. I don't know why, but I feared I might never see her again. We piled into Karen's car and headed to their house.

Steve and I spent the rest of the afternoon playing. Dinner time came and Todd grilled hamburgers. Karen and Todd both seemed a little anxious, as they tried to keep me busy. Late evening rolled around, and I began to think more about Mom. Questioning Karen resulted in the same response: "Sometimes it takes a long time to get the baby out of a mommy's tummy. Grandma will call when the baby is born."

We were getting ready for bed when the phone rang. Karen answered and broke into a big smile. "It's for you." I slowly took the phone and was relieved to hear Mom's voice. I had a baby sister. Mom was feeling good and couldn't wait till I could meet my little sister. I would be spending the night with Todd and Karen. Todd yelled out "party time" as he got out soda and snacks. I don't think anybody was ready for bed.

Mom came home late afternoon the next day. I realized that nobody had told me the baby's name. Oh well, I'd find out soon enough. Mom looked pretty tired as Grandma helped her into the house. Even though it was a hot August day, the baby was wrapped in a blanket, which seemed a little strange to me. Finally, the big moment arrived. I got to see my little sis. I asked her name, but Mom hadn't given her one yet. She wanted some name ideas from me. I don't know why but the name Maggie popped into my head. Mom got a big smile, saying, "Maggie, meet your big sister, Emma." Wow! I got to name my new baby sister.

Getting Back into a Routine

Things started changing around Grandma's house pretty quickly. Mom and Maggie took over Grandma's sewing room, which had moved to the new room in the basement. I stayed in Mom's room which we'd been sharing. Mom went back to work three weeks after Maggie was born. She was pretty tired when she got home, but the sight of Maggie and me usually brought her back to life. A friend of Grandma's, Marie, occasionally watched Maggie and me when Grandma had lots of sewing jobs to complete. Aunt Sally and Uncle Jake were around more, occasionally taking me back to their house for the day. My cousin Max and I got along great. It seemed like Maggie's birth brought us together as a family. It was the best!

The more I saw of my aunt and uncle, the more I wondered what it would be like to have a daddy around. Did Mom miss being married? My aunt, uncle, and Max seemed so happy. They were like a real family. Being teachers, they were off summers and always were going somewhere or doing something. Uncle Jake was a cool guy. He adored his family and was always helping out. Why couldn't Mom find somebody like Uncle Jake? I felt kind of bad for her. I felt kind of bad for me.

Since Maggie's birth, Mom really didn't do anything but go to work and come home. She was always physically fried. I got into the "big sister" role and tried to help with Maggie. For some reason, I started to wonder what it would have been like to have a daddy around to help. Maybe Mom wouldn't be so tired all the time. Occasionally one of her girlfriends stopped by and we still saw Karen's family, but Mom was sort of anchored to Maggie and me at the house.

One afternoon while I was playing in the living room, I heard Mom and Aunt Sally in the kitchen talking about Clint needing to provide money to help raise his kid. I didn't understand. She said something about Mom getting a lawyer to get more money from him. I was completely confused. Why would Daddy have to give Mom money? He wasn't around. Maggie's name also came up. Who was her daddy? Did he even know he had a baby? Why did he think he could get off without paying any money to help raise his daughter? Aunt Sally was doing most of the talking. She got angrier and louder the longer they talked. I remember not getting any of it.

That night, I told Mom I had heard Aunt Sally and her talking about Daddy. We hadn't seen him in a long time. Why were they talking about him? She didn't miss him, did she? What did Aunt Sally mean about Daddy having to give her money to help with me? And what about Maggie's daddy? I didn't even know she had a daddy. Mom said there was nothing to worry about. We're a happy family and things were going great. Not exactly an answer! Why wouldn't she tell me more?

Flashing Lights

Between Thanksgiving and Christmas, I got off the bus to see an ambulance in Grandma's driveway. I quickly ran to the door which was wide open. Marie was in the living room holding Maggie. She motioned for me to come over. I noticed the basement door was open. I could hear voices coming from downstairs. Grandma had fallen. Mom found her when she got home from work. Maggie had been in her bed crying. Mom called Marie after she called the ambulance. They were taking Grandma to the hospital. Mom was the first to come up the steps from the basement. A tear-stained Mom rushed to give me a big hug. It's weird, but I remember she was still in her Diner uniform and smelled like French fries. She was going to the hospital with Grandma while Maggie and I would stay with Marie. Aunt Sally was going to meet her at the hospital.

Mom called around dinner time to let Marie know that they were preparing Grandma for surgery. I had heard the word surgery before, but I didn't know what it meant. Marie told me that the doctors had to fix some parts of Grandma which had been broken from her fall on the basement steps. I wanted to know what needed to be fixed. Marie wasn't sure. Mom called later that night to say she and Aunt Sally were staying at the hospital because the doctors were still working with Grandma. She still wasn't home when Marie announced bedtime. I wanted to wait up for Mom, but it was already late, and I had preschool the next day. Marie said Grandma would be staying in the hospital for a while. I really didn't understand. When Mom went into the hospital to have Maggie, she came home the next day.

School wasn't much fun the next day. I kept thinking about everything. When I got home from preschool, Mom was on the couch feeding Maggie. She saw me and started to cry. Aunt Sally came in from the kitchen and sat on the other side of me. I could tell something was wrong. Mom said that Grandma wasn't coming home. Grandma now lived with Jesus. What did that mean? I knew a little about Jesus because Grandma took me to Sunday School at her church and had taught me a few prayers, but living with Jesus? Was Grandma going to live at the church? Mom sadly shook her head saying Grandma had died. Everyone cried but Maggie, who had fallen asleep while feeding.

Adjustments

I can clearly remember how Mom's mood changed after Grandma died. She was tired before, but now she had no energy at all. Smiles and laughter were rare. Even baby Maggie rarely brought her out of a mood. Several days after the funeral, she started back to work. Marie continued to help with childcare.

I heard Mom telling Karen one afternoon, that if she hadn't gotten pregnant with Maggie, Grandma's sewing room would have remained upstairs, and Grandma wouldn't have fallen. Karen reminded her that Grandma still went to the basement to do laundry and other things, but Mom heard none of it. It was almost like she needed somebody to blame for Grandma's death. She had to blame herself. Mom couldn't accept that accidents happen.

Grandma had something called a will. Mom told me it was a piece of paper where Grandma wrote down what should happen to her things, like the house, car, and furniture, after she died. Even though everything was to be split evenly between Sally and her, Sally wanted Mom to keep Grandma's newer car. Aunt Sally and Uncle Jake wanted Mom to buy Grandma's house. Unfortunately, she made so little money at the Diner that she couldn't afford it. They decided to wait till spring to sell it. That way we would all have some time to get used to life without Grandma. We hoped to move in the summer before kindergarten.

Mom and Aunt Sally started going through Grandma's stuff. Jake fixed little things around the house before it was put up for sale. Max and I helped by trying to entertain Maggie as the adults worked. At times, I wondered if any of this would have happened if there had been a daddy around the house. I don't mean my daddy, Clint, just a daddy who could be there for Mom and us. A daddy with a job would mean more money so maybe we would have bought Grandma's house. You know, like Uncle Jake was there for Aunt Sally and Max.

Starting Over

When Grandma's house sold, Mom found a two-bedroom apartment in a four-family house. We moved several weeks after pre-school ended. I started all day kindergarten at a new school in the fall. Mom quit the Diner and started working as an aide in a nursing home closer to our new place. Although she had to work several weekends a month, her overall schedule was more regular. Marie continued to help with babysitting. Mom quickly became friends with the Krafts from our four-family house. Their sixteen-year-old daughter Jill helped with babysitting. We often spent time with Aunt Sally and Uncle Todd on weekends. Occasionally Mom got a case of the blues when talking about Grandma. I really missed Grandma, but I hated seeing Mom beat herself up because of Grandma's accident. Months had passed and she continued to blame herself for Grandma's fall.

Before you knew it, I was starting first grade. They had a parent-teacher ice cream social one evening several days before school started. The teacher introduced each family. I quickly noticed that most kids had a mom and dad at the ice cream party. I only counted three other kids who only had one parent there. I guessed they were like me. By now, I had grown used to only having a mom at home. The ice cream party might have been the first time I realized other kids also lived with only one parent. First grade went by in a flash.

Summertime

One Saturday we went to a picnic at Aunt Sally's. There were tons of people and kids there whom we'd never met. Most of the adults taught with my aunt and uncle. Maggie and I quickly found kids to play with. As the afternoon turned to evening, I noticed that Mom seemed relaxed and was having fun. It was a great day! I asked Mom on the way home when we were going to see those folks again. I really liked all the kids. Mom explained that they were my aunt and uncle's friends, so we might never see them again. That's not what I wanted to hear.

About a week after the picnic, I noticed a missed call on her cell which she'd laid on the table when we got home from the store. She hit voicemail as we unloaded groceries. "Christa, this is Dale from the picnic last weekend. Your sister gave me your number. I hope you don't mind. I'll call later." Mom stopped in her tracks, just staring at the phone for several seconds before continuing to put away groceries. I couldn't tell what she was thinking. After the groceries were put away, she went to her room and called her sister. I heard her laughing, so I guess she wasn't too upset about Dale's call.

The next day, Dale called again. Mom answered the phone and took it to her bedroom, closing the door. I asked about the call when she came out. She asked whether Maggie or I remembered Dale from the picnic. Neither of us did. I wanted to know what he called for. She was going out with him sometime next weekend if she could get Jill to babysit. I broke into a big grin, asking if Dale was her boyfriend. Mom laughed saying she'd just met the guy.

Dale picked Mom up on Saturday. She looked real nice but seemed anxious as she answered the door. Dale seemed kind of nervous as well. Maggie and I looked him over while Mom made a last trip to her bedroom. They were going to a restaurant where a friend of Dale's played in a band. Mom gave Jill a few last-minute instructions before heading out the door. We went to bed before Mom got home.

Mom was in a great mood the next morning. She called her sister from her bedroom right after breakfast. I heard laughing, lots of laughing. Later that evening, Mom answered the phone again, retreating to her bedroom where she talked forever. When asked, she said she was on the phone with Dale. She planned on going out with him hopefully next weekend. Hmm ... Maybe Dale would become Mom's boyfriend!

Within weeks, Mom and Dale were spending lots of time together. He taught at the high school. He was nice to Maggie and me; however, he didn't always seem comfortable around us. I don't know, maybe little kids just made him nervous. The remainder of the summer and fall were all good. We were invited to his parent's house for Thanksgiving. I'd never been in such a big fancy house. His dad took right to Maggie. It was our best holiday since Grandma had died. When we left, Dale's mom gave us each a big hug, saying she hoped to see us at Christmas. Mom seemed very, very happy. I began to wonder where this was all going. I really liked Dale, but I knew she had been let down by men in the past. Mom didn't pray with us before bedtime like Grandma, but that night, I asked God not to let Mom get hurt.

Christmas

Maggie and I woke early on Christmas to find Santa had left presents under our tree. Maggie pounced on Mom's bed to wake her up. The next several hours were spent enjoying our new gifts. Later we packed into the car and headed to Aunt Sally's for lunch. It was a lot of fun. We got several more gifts and enjoyed the company of family. Around 5:00, we headed to Dale's parent's house for dinner. I don't know if I had ever seen so many Christmas lights on a house. Maggie and I just stood in the driveway staring.

Dale's parents welcomed us with hugs. Christmas music was playing, and everyone appeared happy to see us. His brother Ken and his girlfriend were home from college. Mom went to the kitchen to help with dinner while everyone else entertained Maggie and me. Dinner was just fun. Everyone talked and joked around with each other. I found myself wishing we had a family like this.

After dinner, Dale's dad announced that Santa had left something under the tree for two little girls. Really, how did Santa know we were going to be there? Unfortunately, it got late too soon and we had to drive home. Maggie fell asleep within minutes, but my mind was buzzing. Dale's family was great! Mom seemed to like Dale. Who knows? Maybe she loved him. Could this work out for Mom? Maybe they'd get married and we'd become a family? Maybe God answered my prayers about Mom not getting hurt.

New Year's Eve was spent at home with Mom and Dale. We had special snacks and played games. Both Maggie and I were falling asleep, so they helped us to bed before midnight. The next morning Mom was really silly at breakfast. A little later that morning, I noticed something on her hand. She showed us a ring that Dale had given her after we went to bed. I was pretty sure I knew what that meant. Mom was going to get married. Both Maggie and I jumped up and down. She laughed saying she wondered how long it was going to take for one of us to notice the ring. She was happy that we were happy. Mom had worried that we might not want her to get married. It was the best news we'd heard since Grandma died.

New Beginnings

Dale owned a house close to his school. Mom called it a ranch style house. I initially looked around asking about farm animals, I mean, she said it was a ranch. They both cracked up. The house had three bedrooms and a big basement. The fenced backyard was a great place to play. Mom found a new job at a retirement center just minutes from "our" new home. I was excited. We all were excited.

It was July tenth and it was time to get married. It was a beautiful sunny day, not too hot, but perfect. Maggie and I got fancy dresses, and we got to walk down the aisle with Aunt Sally. A big party followed with a DJ, food, and all the soda you could drink. Maggie and I danced and danced and danced. It was the best party I had ever been to. Mom and Dale went away for several days to the Smoky Mountains so we stayed with Aunt Sally.

With the move came school number three. After signing papers in the school office, we took a tour. It was huge. I worried a little bit about getting lost.

Number Three

I heard Mom throwing up in the morning several months after their honeymoon. Something seemed familiar, but I wasn't sure what. Finally, Mom and Dale sat us down to announce they were having a baby. Didn't they mean that Mom was going to have a baby? I laid in bed that night thinking, wow, another kid around the house. I wasn't sure how I felt about it. Maggie was finally to the age where she could do lot of things herself. She was fun. I guess we were starting over again with a new baby due in April.

Dale's parents were crazy happy. This was their first infant grandchild. They had called themselves Grandma and Grandpa around Maggie and me since the wedding, but I could tell this was different. When we told Aunt Sally, she responded with a big smile, joking "That was quick." Mom rolled her eyes and laughed. I had no idea what that was about. The idea of a baby was beginning to sink in. Everyone was so happy so I decided I should be too.

Over the next few months, we began to look and act more like a family. We did more things together and I really liked living in a house again. My new school was nice and I quickly found out that several classmates lived nearby. I played on a soccer team that fall. Everybody, including Dale's parents, came to my games. Mom gradually got bigger and more tired. Dale chipped in to help with things like cooking, laundry, shopping and housework. Grandma and Grandpa treated Mom like she was their daughter. Both Maggie and I got really excited one day when Mom put our hands on her belly to feel the baby kick. The retirement home allowed Mom to work part-time the month before she was due. There was fun filled excitement in the air.

Thursday, April tenth, started like any other day. Dale and I both went off to school. Mom was off work, so Maggie stayed home with her. I got home to find Grandma and Grandpa with Maggie. Dale and Mom had left for the hospital after lunch. She would have the baby soon. Our grandparents tried to keep us busy. Suppertime rolled around and still no word. Grandpa ordered pizza, but nobody was very hungry. Maggie wondered out loud whether we were going to have a sister or a brother. We passed time thinking of possible boy and girl names for the baby. They let us stay up late because I was off school the next day for Easter break. By ten o'clock, Maggie had fallen asleep on the couch. I don't know how much longer I lasted, but I awoke as Grandpa tucked me into bed. Still no word from the hospital.

Maggie and I woke early on Friday. Grandma and Grandpa were already in the kitchen drinking coffee. They broke into big smiles when they saw us. I knew why, but I'm not sure

Maggie did. They had Mom's phone number at the hospital where she awaited our call. Grandpa couldn't dial the number quick enough. We had a baby sister who was born at 3:15 in the morning. Maggie wanted to know the name. As when Maggie was born, no name had been picked yet. Our grandparents took us to visit Mom and the baby after lunch. She would be coming home Saturday, just in time for Easter. After we got home from the hospital, Grandma said this was truly a "Good Friday!"

Not long after they got home, Grandpa had the five of us sit on the couch for our first "family photo." Family, yeah, that's what Grandpa called it. Mom kept referring to our little sister as baby. Maggie said she needed a name. Dale asked for our suggestions. Obviously, Maggie had given it some thought as she quickly chimed in: "Simon." Mom chuckled, wanting to know where she came up with that name, while telling her Simon was a boy's name. Maggie said it was her favorite chipmunk from the cartoon show. Everyone laughed. Mom looked at Dale and said, how about Simone, a girl version of Simon. He looked at their baby, kidding about her chubby chipmunk cheeks and said, "Simone it is!"

Mom started calling Dale, "Dad." I remember feeling a little weird hearing this. He had always been Dale to everyone before Simone was born. Near the end of spring break week, we were all at the kitchen table for breakfast. I don't know what came over me, but I said, "Dad, can you pour me some juice?" They looked at each other and grinned. Now we were definitely a family. Maggie who always followed my lead, quickly fell in line calling Dale Dad.

Again????

Every summer, Dad built decks several days a week with A.J., a fellow teacher. I noticed he was gone a lot the summer before sixth grade. One morning, Mom took a call from A. J.. She thought Dad was out working with him, but A.J. said he'd been on vacation for two weeks. She had a puzzled look on her face as she hung up the phone. That night I heard a monster argument coming from their room. Dad was gone before I got up the next morning.

Mom was in a bad mood as she drove us to Aunt Sally's while she went to work. She kept talking to herself and I noticed a tear running down her face as we got out of the car. What had happened? I began to worry. Aunt Sally didn't answer any of my questions when I tried to ask what was going on with Mom. Several phone calls were made between Mom and Aunt Sally that day. Uncle Jake tried to keep us busy, but even he seemed a little out of it. It was like all the adults were trying to keep a big secret from Maggie and me. Mom's mood hadn't improved when she picked us after work. She pretty much ignored us all evening. What had Dad done?

Things got nasty real quick. Dad moved out by the end of the summer. Grandma and Grandpa didn't know what to do. We had become very close. What a mess! What happened to "our family?" Mom's mood was ugly. She was cranky and had a short temper with everyone. Mom ranted one evening to Aunt Sally about where we would live. Dad rarely came around the house after he moved out. Sometimes we saw him at our grandparent's house on weekends. It wasn't much fun. Grandma kept trying to act like everything was normal, but it wasn't. I think she expected them to patch things up. Maybe she feared losing her grandchildren. At our grandparent's, Dale spent most of his time with Simone, which was fine with me. I started calling him Dale again. I was mad, things had been good and now they were lousy. Maggie didn't get it.

A few months into the school year, Mom pulled me aside to tell me they were getting a divorce. Dale had a girlfriend and didn't love her anymore. I'd heard enough talk around the house that I already knew about his fellow track coach girl-friend. We'd probably have to move, but she did not know where to or when. I cried. I don't know if it was because I was sad, angry or what. I hated seeing Mom this way. The thought of moving was upsetting. For the last several years we had a normal family, with a mom, dad, siblings and loving grand-parents. I was angry, really, really angry, because none of this would have happened if Dale still loved Mom! Why did he need a girlfriend? Mom did not display any emotion as we talked. She'd talk to Maggie later that day.

During spring break, we moved into a small apartment in a house pretty close to Aunt Sally. Happy birthday Simone! It was a different neighborhood which meant we had to change schools, again. Changing schools is hard. Changing schools with six weeks left in the school year is harder. Mom tried to be positive, but it really didn't work. I don't know if I didn't like my new teacher, or if I was just mad about changing schools, or what! I had never been in trouble at school until now. I got into a big fight because a girl wouldn't let me play soccer at recess. I was just glad to get the school year over.

Our New Life

So we were back to the four of us, in a small apartment, in a new school. Mom was always whipped. She wasn't the same mom she had been when married to Dale. Looking back, I realize that she'd been depressed. I'd seen her that way near the end with Clint, occasionally when she was pregnant with Maggie, when Grandma died, and now with the divorce. I sometimes heard her crying at night and when she was on the phone. Thank God for her sister Sally and her family. They did things together often while Jake frequently took us with him and Max. That first year after the divorce was rough.

Dale visited Simone every other weekend at his parent's house. Since Maggie and I weren't his kids, we didn't go. Although I didn't remember Clint, I sometimes wondered why he didn't visit me. I don't think I was jealous of Simone and Dale, but I felt I was missing something, even if I couldn't exactly tell you what that something was. His parents kept in touch and came over to visit occasionally the first year after the divorce. I got the feeling that they were both mad at their son for what he had put us through. Mom didn't blame them. I think she missed them but seeing them reminded her of the life we all once had, the family we once were.

I guess I didn't help much either. The end of sixth grade in a new school didn't go well, and seventh grade wasn't much better. I had been pretty popular at my old school, but I just couldn't seem to break in at the new place. My grades fell and I got into trouble for a lot of little things. A lot of little things turned into a big thing. There were phone calls home and several conferences. I was embarrassed. Mom was mad! One evening, she came into my room and let me have it. She'd never gotten so mad at me before. She went on and on about how hard it was for her to raise three kids by herself. I had let her down. Mom expressed guilt over the divorce, wondering aloud whether it played a role in my school behavior. I didn't know what to say. By the end, we both were in tears. Something had to change. The something was me. I laid low the last quarter of seventh grade. It was kind of lonely.

Eighth grade year was different. I took chorus and joined the vocal performing group. It didn't take long and I had new friends. Grades were back and I looked forward to school. I really liked my math and science teachers who talked me into joining the Girls In Science club. School was good again.

Mom took a new job at the retirement community in the admissions department. This seemed to brighten her outlook. I'm guessing she was making a little more money because we were doing more things. She hoped to look for a little bigger place to live. No down spells in a while.

Our Family

So this is our family – three kids with three dads. Except for Dale seeing Simone, we never saw the other two dads. I sometimes wondered about Maggie's dad. Had Mom been dating him? Was it Gerald? Was it a one-night stand? (I'm in the ninth grade so I know about that.) Uncle Jake always stood in for Dad at dad-daughter events, but it wasn't quite the same. I knew of other kids from school who didn't live with both parents, but I never talked to them about it. Sometimes I wished we could have talked, you know, shared our experiences. Did they feel the way I felt? Did we share some of the same types of experiences? How did they cope? Did they ever feel like life happened to them, that they had very little control? Did they sometimes feel alone, like they had to figure life out on their own?

Sometimes at night I think about what my life would have been like if Clint had been a good guy, like Uncle Jake. However, if Clint had been a great husband, and they had stayed together, there would have been no Maggie and Simone. I can't imagine life without them. Dale, I don't know what to say about him. Everybody had been so happy. We had looked and acted like my friend's families. Dale's parents, Grandma and Grandpa, were the best. I think about them often. We were a family! He hurt us all, especially Mom.

Right now, things seem to be going okay. I know there will be problems in the future, but what the heck, we've worked through problems before. I know my mom struggles, and I believe at times she is lonely. I don't think she has gone out with any guy since divorcing Dale. I don't know if she ever will. Sometimes, when I think about my crazy family's past, I remember a song Mom used to sing around the house after Maggie was born: "We Are Family," by Sister Sledge. Yes, we are!

Sean

My name is Sean, I'm thirteen years old. I have three siblings, Marsha fifteen, Bobby eleven, and Sue eight. I just started my eighth-grade year. We all attend Catholic schools. My mom is a dental hygienist and Dad works in an office downtown. I guess you could say we lived a pretty normal middle-income life in the burbs. We have a four-bedroom house with a two-car garage. We go to church on Sunday and vacation every summer. The local swim club is our hang out. Things are always busy with sports, lessons, and school activities.

Oh What A Night

I'll never forget January 25, sixth-grade year. My parents wanted to talk to all of us in the family room. Were we moving? Had somebody lost a job? Mom was way too old to have another baby, wasn't she? Could Mom or Dad be sick? Nobody acted sick. Maybe they'd booked a Disney Cruise for spring break. Neither Mom nor Dad looked happy. This was not going to be good. They sat on opposite sides of the room, apparently not knowing how to start. Finally, Mom broke the silence saying Dad was moving out this weekend. You could have heard a pin drop. We looked back and forth at each other without saying a word. Sue finally asked, "What do you mean? Dad lives here. Where is he going?" They just didn't get along anymore, and it would be better for everyone if he moved out. The word "shocked" would have been an understatement. What did he mean, "didn't get along anymore." I never saw anything like this coming. Sure, they had their occasional arguments, but doesn't everybody? Dad was moving in with his brother Tony. The kids would be staying with Mom. Marsha bolted, slamming her bedroom door. Sue hugged Mom and started to cry. Bobby grumbled to himself as he walked off to our bedroom. Dad patted my shoulder saying, "We'll work everything out," and left. How are "we" going to do that?

Bobby had headphones on holding a video game controller as I entered our room. A game was on, but Bobby was staring blindly at the monitor. I sat on my bed for a minute before approaching him. He just looked at me, took the headphones off, and left. He returned a short while later, got his pajamas on and hopped into bed, covering his head. I said something like "Dad would be back in no time. We'd work everything out." Crap, where had I just heard that line? I don't think I believed it as I spoke it. Bobby wasn't crying, but he seemed to be talking to himself under the covers.

I went downstairs to get a snack but ended up hardly taking a bite. Went to the family room, but that was too much like revisiting the scene of the crime. It was only 8:30, way too early for bed. I returned to the kitchen but just sat there staring. Mom appeared and sat down. Neither of us knew what to say.

She had been with Sue who had just fallen asleep. Looking teary eyed, she said I could ask her anything. I looked at her for the longest time in silence. I stood, shook my head asking "Why?" as I left the kitchen. I could hear her crying as I started up the steps.

The light was still on in Marsha's room. I hesitated but knocked. She yelled "go away." I identified myself and she let me in. Marsha had been crying. After a few minutes of eyeing each other, she burst out with endless questions. Did you know anything about this? I never heard them fighting much, did you? You don't think Dad had an affair, do you? Mom always talks about the dentist Bart, at her office. You don't think she and Bart ... You don't think any of us are to blame, do you? Do you think they'll be able to afford tuition if they get divorced? There are four kids, school costs a fortune. Will we ever go on a vacation again? Will we have to move? God, if we move, I'll probably have to share a room with Sue. I'll never have any privacy. I'm in eighth grade. I can't have a six-year-old around all the time. I hate them both! Why did they have to do this to us? Marsha rambled on for some time. I couldn't get a word in edgewise. Eventually she appeared emotionally drained. She jumped up and gave me a long hug. That never happens. I headed back to my room feeling numb.

Bobby seemed to be asleep. I was emotionally spent, but I wasn't sleepy as I laid in bed staring at the ceiling, sort of in an emotional daze. I have no idea what time I finally dozed off, but I felt exhausted when the alarm went off for school.

A Good Breakfast to Start Each Day

Mom had waffles, sausage, cereal, bananas, and juice on the table. This only happened occasionally and never during the week. Nobody looked very hungry. Nobody looked very awake. Mom tried to keep things upbeat, asking what we had on for the day. "Nothing" was the common response. We generally kept our eyes focused on the table, eating very little. Marsha came down and was out the door before anyone could say anything. I wondered if Dad spent the night at the house.

When I came down for school, Sue was on Mom's lap still in her pajamas. Sue complained she didn't feel good. Having already taken her temperature, Mom said she would be fine when she saw her friends at school. Sue would have none of it. She cried saying she was about to throw up. Bobby came down, looked at us and headed out the door for the bus. I joined him within minutes. We left without Sue. We took our seats without saying a word. Almost everyone was off the bus before I even realized we were at school.

School

I was exhausted at school. I couldn't get last night out of my head. What was going to happen to us? I replayed Marsha's questions over and over. I had not prepared for a social studies test which I screwed up big time. My math teacher called my name several times before I responded. Classmates laughed. After class, she asked if I was okay, or did I need to see the nurse. I smiled, saying that I was just tired. From the look on her face, I'm not convinced she believed me.

Lunch and recess were my favorite parts of the school day. I didn't have much of an appetite and didn't get into the usual clowning around at our table. My best friend Nick noticed. On the way out to recess, he asked if I was okay. "Perfect!" Nick reacted, "And bears don't poop in the woods either." At recess, I stood with the guys who never play sports. Nick glanced over, shaking his head several times during the basketball game.

I dreaded running into Mom when I got home. What could I say to her? Oh, so you and Dad don't like each other anymore, that's cool with me. So Mom, who's to blame, you or Dad? Like how did you decide who should move out? Did you play rock, paper scissors? Did you guys think about the kids when you made this wonderful decision to split? How long have you and Dad not been "getting along?" You know this was like dropping a bomb on us!

Luckily Mom was still at work when we arrived home. A note on the fridge said Sue was at Grandma's. After changing clothes, Bobby came down to get something to eat. I asked about school, and he angrily said he'd gotten points for not having his homework done. I grinned, he grinned. Bobby said, "This is bullshit!" I'd never heard him use that word before. I started to laugh. "Bullshit, bullshit, bullshit!" we cried out. Neither of us could stop laughing. We retreated to our room and played video games, something we hadn't done together in a long time. That night we came up with a secret code. If either of us thought something was bullshit, we'd say "*SB*."

Mom arrived home with a healthy-looking Sue. I get it. She was really upset and probably felt crummy before school. Marsha, Bobby, and I probably all felt the same. Sue did what little kids do. You feel lousy. You beg your parents to stay home. "I'm going to throw up" works almost every time. Sue had a great day at Grandma's. I was a little jealous.

I think all of us wondered if Dad would be home for dinner. Marsha called saying she was at her friend's house for the evening. Sue eventually asked about Dad. We stared at Mom. Dad called Mom earlier to say he was going out with friends after work. In a sarcastic tone, Bobby blurted, "Welcome to the new normal!" Mom bit her lip as she gazed out the window. We ate in silence, even Sue.

The Move

Mom and Dad were both busy Saturday morning. Neither parent paid much attention as we got ourselves cereal. Marsha, as usual, was still in bed. By the time we'd dressed, Dad was carrying clothes to his car. Initially I felt I should offer to help, but something inside me wouldn't allow it. Bobby took off to our room, probably losing his mind in video games. Sue looked completely confused and headed to the basement where Mom was doing laundry. I got madder and madder, while avoiding eye contact with Dad. He asked that I tell Mom he'd be back later to get a few more things. As he walked out the door, I yelled, "Tell her yourself!"

Marsha eventually emerged from her room asking what was up. When I told her, she shook her head numerous times, went to the kitchen, grabbed something to eat, and headed back to her room, slamming the door. I really didn't know what to do with myself. Everyone was in their own place – Sue with Mom in the basement, Bobby in our room, Marsha in her room, and Dad was at Uncle Tony's. Although I love basketball, my 3:00 game was of little interest. I turned on the TV, but I couldn't tell you what was on.

Dad arrived back around 12:45. We had just sat down for lunch. Sue excitedly asked him to join us. Everyone's eyes went to Mom. They looked at each other. Neither of them said a word. Sue repeated her request. He looked at Sue with a forced smile, saying he was sorry, but he was in a hurry. He took off up the stairs to retrieve more stuff. Everyone except Sue seemed relieved. Sue looked puzzled as she asked why Dad wouldn't eat with us. She obviously didn't grasp this Dad moving out thing. The rest of us said nothing, busying ourselves with eating. Dad avoided the kitchen as he brought down bags of clothes. I cleaned up while Mom and Sue went to the family room. I could hear them talking about what had occurred in the last two days. I remember hearing Sue begging Mom to "Make Dad move back." Mom tried to reassure her that things would turn out all right.

Week One (minus) Dad

The next week was really weird. Dad's absence was the invisible presence that hovered over our house. With Monday, came our weekly routines of school, team practices and other activities. Nobody, I mean nobody, brought up Dad or what might have happened between them. Mom was more scattered than ever. She tried to put on a happy face at meals, but it didn't seem real. I was mad, but I didn't know where to direct my anger. Should I be mad at Mom? Should I be mad at Dad? Should I be mad at both of them? Sometimes I felt like I just wanted to hit something. My basketball coach pulled me aside after practice and joked that aggressive play was good, but please don't injure our whole team before our next game.

I don't know if Mom was feeling guilty or what, but on Friday she brought us to the family room after dinner. I remember thinking, "Is Mom going to tell us she's moving out?" We sat waiting for her to say something. She started talking about how difficult the last week had been for all of us. She admitted that she had not been herself, and everyone seemed to be "walking on eggshells." (I explained walking on eggshells to Sue.) Mom looked as if she might break into tears at any moment.

Marsha interrupted Mom to ask the big question that had been on all of our minds.: "What happened between you and Dad? Everything seemed to be fine. You guys never got into big fights!"

Mom nodded, agreeing that they really didn't fight. After a pause, Mom said they had not been getting along for a long time. She didn't give much of an explanation as to why. "People sometimes just grow apart. There was no real big issue that split us up, there were just lots of little things."

Sue whined, "I miss Daddy." It all seemed like crap to me. How do you fall out of love after all those years and four kids?

Mom went on to say she didn't have a clear picture of the near future. She had wanted to try marriage counseling, but Dad had refused. Marsha grumbled "I guess Dad doesn't want to get back together. Maybe he doesn't love us anymore either!" Sue began to cry. Mom brought her over to sit on her lap. She reassured us that Dad still loved all of us. This was between them, the kids had nothing to do with it. "Why had we not heard from him since last Saturday?" Mom shook her head. She pointed out we'd have to pitch in a bit more with chores. She teased Marsha that she might even have to learn how to cook. Marsha was not amused. Sue quickly volunteered that she wanted to cook dinner. Everyone except Bobby cracked up. Sue couldn't even reach the microwave which was above the stove. Were we doomed to peanut butter sandwiches seven days a week?

We spent the evening eating popcorn and watching a movie. Bobby, who had yet to utter a sound, went to our room. The evening was okay. I realized Mom was as confused about our new situation as we were. There were so many unanswered questions. The future was so unclear. I wasn't sure how I felt about any of it, but at least it had been a start.

Dad Time #1

I was the lucky one to take Dad's call on Saturday. He immediately apologized for not seeing us all week. I didn't respond. What did he expect me to say? No big deal Dad. You guys just screwed up our lives, but we'll handle it. Great to hear from you though. How's your week been? Mine has been fantastic! I told Mom he had called and wanted to take the kids out somewhere. She thought it was a good idea to go, yet it was our decision. Heck, I didn't know if I wanted to see him. After last night, I found myself more mad, frustrated, and confused about Dad. I kept thinking about him turning down marriage counseling. Had he given up on Mom? Giving up on her felt a little like he was also giving up on his kids.

Dad stopped by at 11:45 Sunday to pick us up. My parents said very little to each other. Sue ran to give him a hug. The ride to the restaurant was a little weird. No one, including Dad, said much of anything. At the restaurant Dad asked non-stop questions about each of our weeks as we waited for our food. It was strange. I don't ever remember him taking such an interest in our activities in the past. It seemed over the top to me. Bobby barely responded to his questions. Marsha and I were polite but not overly engaged. Sue was the only one who readily spoke with him. Actually, Sue was the only one who seemed happy to be there.

Finally, lunch was over, and we could go sit in a quiet theater with no more questions. Dad asked what we wanted from the concession counter at the theater. This was new. We never bought snacks at the movies. He always complained about the cost, so Mom usually brought a few things from home. Sue picked the movie and Bobby sat as far away from Dad as possible. The ride home was relatively uneventful. Dad pulled in the drive and switched from Mom's minivan to his car. Sue asked if he was coming in for dinner. He gave some lame excuse about being busy. Even Sue questioned what he had to do on Sunday night. It was good to be home. Thank God Mom didn't ask us any questions about our outing. I don't know why, but our lunch and movie with Dad had been exhausting.

My BF

Nick had been my best friend since first grade. We spent time at each other's houses and played on teams together. His parents treated me like family and my parents did the same with him. Up to now, I hadn't told Nick anything about what had happened. Maybe I was just hoping it would all go away. Dad would return, and everything would go back to the way it was. After Mom's family talk on Friday night, and the outing with Dad on Sunday, I had serious doubts that anything would ever be the same.

One Wednesday, we hung out in Nick's basement playing video games. Nick quickly noticed that I was not into it. He put his controller down, looked me in the eye, demanding to know what was going on. I told him everything, starting with the family meeting almost two weeks ago. I was surprised how easy it was to tell him after I got started. I thought I'd be embarrassed but I wasn't. Nick asked questions and I answered. When I was all talked out, Nick shook his head angrily saying, "That sucks!" I couldn't have agreed more. I told Nick he could tell his parents, but no one else. I felt relieved to get it off my chest.

Scheduling

About six weeks after Dad moved, Mom told us he wanted a regular scheduled time to see us. A schedule to see Dad? Since when do you make a schedule to see your father? I mean, really, this was crazy! She believed Sundays would be best because we rarely had games or other activities; however, she wanted our input. Marsha complained about missing things with friends if she had to see Dad every Sunday. She also griped that our first several visits were boring. There was nothing to talk about, and Dad wouldn't stop with the questions.

Mom turned to Bobby, who looked at the floor and said nothing. Mom pushed, trying for some input from him. Bobby looked straight at Mom for several seconds, then looked at me and mouthed SB. I had to bite my tongue to keep from laughing.

Sue seemed to enjoy our visits with Dad the most. Mom's questions to Sue, were answered by questions from Sue. "Why did Dad have to move out?" "Don't you like each other anymore?" "Doesn't Dad miss me?" Mom didn't answer, appearing tired as she slowly looked at each of us.

Mom looked at me after a period of awkward silence. I didn't know what to say, but I was on the hot seat. I agreed with Marsha. I said our visits hadn't been much fun. I missed Dad somedays, but on other days, I was so mad that I was glad he wasn't around. Marsha nodded in agreement. We should be allowed to skip weekly visits if we had something else going on. Marsha nodded again. Mom didn't react one way or another, saying she and Dad would be speaking in the next several days to figure something out.

No big surprise, Sunday visits won. I guess that meant more movies and restaurants. With such a large age gap, it became harder to find an appropriate movie we all wanted to see. Hopefully we could do something outdoors when spring arrived. Mom told us we could skip a visit if we had something really "big or important" to do. Marsha asked her to define "big and important." She said nothing. I wondered whether Dad really wanted to see us, or was this just something he felt he had to do? When I told Nick of the schedule, he suggested Dad was trying to win points in case they ever got divorced and he'd have to go before a judge. I'd never thought of that. Would he do such a thing? My few positive feelings towards him became more clouded.

Unnatural Visitation

No one dared try the "something big or important to do" excuse the first week. A trip to the natural history museum had been planned. Thank God, no movie. Sue often took Dad's hand while Marsha constantly looked at her phone as we walked around the museum. Bobby remained relatively quiet and I guess you could say I tried to be polite. The afternoon was okay.

The next several months went pretty much the same. Dad tried to find other things for us to do. (Mom must have told him.) Occasionally Marsha or I had something else on. Dad continued to ask about school and our teams. We rarely talked in the car. Marsha listened to music with ear buds and Bobby played electronic games. I stared out the window a lot.

There was something unnatural about Dad's behavior. For example, he frequently offered to buy us stuff. Once he bought us zoo sweatshirts at forty-five dollars a pop. Who was he trying to impress? He was constantly offering ice cream and other snacks. You had to know Dad to recognize how weird this behavior was. Mom was always the one who convinced him to spend a little money on fun stuff. Within weeks Marsha recognized what was going on. She perfected the art of getting Dad to open his wallet. I guess I shouldn't complain, as we all benefited from Marsha's conniving behavior.

Mom told us that she was going to spend Sunday with her friend Clair. We would spend the day at the house with Dad.

No one objected. After lunch he suggested board games, but only Sue showed interest. We all went about our own business while they played several games. Marsha was in her room, Bobby played video games while I did a little homework and watched TV. Dad spent a fair amount of time in the basement and garage. I didn't know what he was doing, and I really didn't care. It was like he was there, but he wasn't. At least we didn't have to pile into the minivan to do something for the sake of doing something. Although Mom wasn't around, this was more the way Sundays used to be. Everybody kind of did their own thing. What I feared was going to be a stressful day, turned out to be okay.

Carrying several bags Mom and Claire arrived home by 7:30. Mom seemed happier than I had seen her in ages. Clair glared at Dad as he got ready to leave. It seemed obvious that Clair knew more about the split up than any of us. I watched out the window as Mom walked out to the car with Dad. They spoke for a few minutes. Neither of them showed any emotion. Mom didn't ask about our day. That was okay with me.

Dad's Apartment

Dad moved out of Uncle Tony's in July. His move signaled that their separation might be permanent. No big surprise. Mom and Dad rarely spoke in person anymore.

Marsha waved me into her room wanting to know what I thought about him getting his own place. I didn't know what to say. I remember her saying, "Divorce, they are going to get a divorce. I knew they were going to get a divorce. I just knew it." Hearing Marsha say the "*D*" word brought buried feelings to the surface. I had been trying to deny the real possibility of divorce for months. I'm not sure who started to cry first, but tears were flowing. We talked. We'd yet to hear either parent mention divorce. We wanted to ask Mom but were scared of what she might say. Mom had been in a pretty good mood for some time, and neither of us wanted to upset her.

Dad took us to his place the following Sunday. It was the second floor of a two-family house. It had two bedrooms, a big kitchen, and a living room with a balcony which overlooked the front yard. Dad was excited about his new place. We could come over anytime and maybe sleep over in a few weeks. He planned on buying several bunk beds. Sue was excited. Bobby said nothing. Marsha looked at me rolling her eyes. I just nodded, not sure what to say. My mind was racing as I pictured four kids on bunk beds in one small bedroom. As we left, I guessed two of us were going to have many days with "something big or important" to do.

Dad got serious about changing our visitation schedule now that he had his own place. He wanted one weekend day and a weekday evening visit. Dad also wanted us to stay overnight sometimes on Saturday. This was getting crazy. We had our lives. The Sunday get togethers weren't always great, but we had gotten used to them. Now there were occasional sleepovers and a weekday evening visit. No, none of this sounded good to me. The only person who didn't seem to mind was Sue. Bobby looked at Mom, shook his head, and looked at me mumbling *SB* as he headed off. Marsha immediately asked what Mom thought. Mom liked the plan we had been using for nearly seven months. She would talk to Dad. Were we finally going to see them fight? I secretly hoped so!

There was more than a little tension playing putt-putt golf the next Sunday. We didn't know if he had spoken with Mom yet. Upon returning to his place, Dad went on and on about how much he missed us. He talked about all the great times we could have if we could only see each other more. After several minutes of rambling, Marsha headed to the bathroom where she stayed for around fifteen minutes. During that time, no one said much of anything. Dad changed the subject, but a sour mood hung over the room. Marsha emerged from the bathroom saying she was sick and needed to go home. It was the longest, quietest, twenty-minute drive I'd ever taken. Mom met us at the door and immediately knew something had happened. She probably suspected he had talked to us about visiting.

Nick and Mom Weigh In

Nick, who always gave his opinion, was pissed that I couldn't hang with him on Sundays. He believed they were headed for a divorce. Nick used to get along with Dad, but now he referred to him as "the jerk." I agreed with most of what he said, but it didn't feel right coming from somebody else. Except for Marsha, I'd never heard anyone talk so negatively about him. Nick thought my mom was way cool. He asked why she hadn't dumped him yet. I didn't have an answer. He asked if Mom had gotten a lawyer. I'd never thought of that. The more he talked, the more worried and confused I became. Where was my family headed? Would I be happier if they divorced? How would a divorce change things? I mean we'd still have to visit him. I didn't know how I felt about Dad anymore. I was glad when we headed off to shoot hoops.

One Saturday Mom sat down as I watched TV. She sensed I had not been myself lately, and gently asked what was going on. She didn't push, but I finally let it out. Mom held to her story that they had drifted apart over the years. Nothing specific had happened. There was no other man, and she did not think Dad had an affair. She did not hate Dad, but she didn't love him anymore either. She knew only Sue enjoyed the visits. Mom had no idea why Dad didn't show up to more games. Divorce had been on her mind for several months. She had not contacted a lawyer but had thought about it. I shared some of what Nick had told me about divorce. She listened closely and confirmed much of what Nick had said. If Mom had been thinking about divorce, I guess it might happen. I wondered if Dad thought about divorce. I asked what happens if one person wants a divorce and the other person doesn't. Mom half-smiled, saying "that's when things can get tricky." What did she mean by tricky? "That's when lawyers make lots of money." I didn't understand what she meant.

It Happened ... Sort of

Dad eventually demanded more regularly scheduled time with the kids. I overheard Mom arguing with him on the

133

phone late one night when going to the bathroom. It sounded like she stood up for our wants. Dad was moody the next several visits, not trying to hide the fact that he was upset with something. Was that something us? Did he feel betrayed by his kids? Should I feel guilty? I didn't. I wasn't exactly happy with him either.

I returned from school to find Mom at the kitchen table staring at a letter. I don't think she realized I came in. I noticed she'd been crying. Dad had a lawyer send a letter about seeing the kids more often. Our divorce talk came back to mind. It looked like Dad fired the first shot. Mom admitted it could be the initial step in what could end in a divorce. Mom quickly gathered up the letter asking that I not tell my siblings. She would tell everyone as soon as she had more information. That was a heavy load to lay on me. Why me?

A week later, Mom talked to Marsha and me about Dad, his lawyer, and the visiting issue. Mom had met with a lawyer for advice. Her lawyer was going to set up a meeting to see if they could work things out. Marsha angrily wanted to know why she was telling us this since we weren't going to have any say in what happened. Marsha grumbled, "Lawyers, I guess it's finally happening. You're getting a divorce." Mom said she didn't know. With downcast eyes in barely audible voice, Marsha asked if she wanted a divorce. After a brief pause, Mom shrugged. "I don't think we can go on like this forever. Something has to happen. I guess I've just been denying it."

Mom, Dad, and the lawyers met to work things out. I was confident Mom would get her way. Her expression suggested things didn't work out the way we had hoped. We were going to try something new for several months. Dad would ask Mom by Wednesday if he wanted to have us for a sleepover on Saturday, rather than a regular Sunday afternoon visit. We didn't have to go if we had "something big" going on. Mom convinced Dad that four kid sleepovers in one small bedroom was a problem. He agreed to have the guys one night and the girls another. We would also try a weekly Wednesday evening visit. Initially, nobody said a thing, but as we were leaving the room, Sue shouted, "So we get to see Dad more?" Bobby nudged me and whispered *SB*. After mom left, Marsha said, "My room."

Marsha was mad as hell. She blamed Mom for not sticking up for us. Marsha had no plans of spending the night with Dad and Sue. What would they do, play board games, and watch stupid DVDs Sue liked? Marsha wanted to come up with a plan to sabotage everything. She would find an activity which met on Wednesday nights. She ranted how she had perfected faking sickness which she wouldn't hesitate to use.

Although frustrated and let down by Mom, she was really furious with Dad. Was he trying to ruin her whole life? I still wasn't sure how I felt about Dad. I really didn't miss him. I often told myself I loved him, however, was I just saying that because he was my dad? As I was about to leave Marsha's room, she moaned, "You know they are going to get a divorce, don't you?" I asked if that's what she wanted. Marsha yelled,

135

"Just get that @#$@#$@ man out of my life. He's @#$@#$ up everything, Mom, you, me, all of us!" I headed out the door walking around the neighborhood to nearly dark, just needing to get away.

Dad Time #2

We started the new schedule the next week. Dad arrived on Sunday with plans of going to the zoo. The weather forecast was rain, but he insisted we go, suggesting a little rain never hurt anybody. A little rain, haaa! Within a half hour, the sky opened up. After seeking shelter in a hot stuffy exhibit building, we made the long dash to the car. Marsha sarcastically remarked that we should each gather up animals for the ark. Dad shot her an angry look. I laughed. Nobody said a word in the car. He took us straight home since we were soaked. Mom rolled her eyes as we entered the garage. Dad quickly switched cars and took off.

On Wednesday we stopped for carry-out on the way to his apartment. We watched TV while Bobby played hand-held video games. Dad looked tired, putting off Sue when she tried to get him to play Uno. I think he realized the first Wednesday visit was a flop, so he stopped for ice cream on the way home. As I got a drink before bed, Mom asked how it went. I shrugged, saying okay. I think she knew the real answer.

Temperature Rising

Mom and Clair sat in the family room sharing a bottle of wine one night. As they got louder, I sat on the stairs and listened. Mom complained about money. She'd gotten a call from the bank saying they were late on their house payment, which I guess had always been taken care of by Dad. She had never been so embarrassed. I wasn't sure about the bank stuff, but it sounded serious. The monthly check from Dad to help with expenses had gotten smaller. She complained about him using her mini-van but feared pushing him to get a bigger car of his own because of money problems. Mom worried about Catholic school tuition. She wasn't crazy about our public school district. She feared we couldn't afford to move to a better public school district if he didn't come up with our Catholic school tuition for next year. I'd never considered the possibility of moving, much less going to a public school. Her lawyer suggested she needed a legal document to protect the kids as well as herself. I didn't understand what that meant. Dad never abused us, what did we need protection from? Everything had just entered a new phase.

I tossed and turned for hours that night. I had come to accept that they were probably never going to get back together, but couldn't they see what this was doing to us? By now I believed we all blamed Dad for the current mess. I didn't even care why they split up anymore. I just wanted things to settle down. I really began to feel for Mom. She was trying to hold things together, but I could tell it was killing her. All she did was work, come home, do laundry, cook, clean, and play taxi driver getting us to our various activities. We tried to pitch in to help. Mom always looked whipped and recently she started complaining about putting on weight. Her only outlet was her nightly phone calls with Clair and their occasional get togethers.

A Few More Bumps

Marsha started hanging out with a different group of kids the summer before freshman year. She was wearing black outfits and dark make-up. Marsha dyed her brown hair black with streaks of red. Bobby asked if she was going as a witch at a Halloween party. Mom just rolled her eyes and calmly told her they'd talk. Dad voiced his disgust with her new fashion statement. Her grades tanked first quarter. Dad blamed Mom for losing control of Marsha. He wanted to lower the hammer! Several evenings later, Mom and Marsha came from the basement and her hair color was back to normal. They were both laughing. She wasn't Dad's sweet little girl anymore.

Bobby was always a clever, funny kid; however, his humor became more sarcastic after Dad moved. Bobby was also the family whiz kid. He never opened a book or studied for a test yet got straight A's. After Dad left, he rarely completed home and classroom assignments, yet reminded us that he aced all tests. Bobby feared what might happen between Mom and Dad at a teacher requested conference. Would Dad lose it and say some really stupid things? Being the logical older brother, I suggested he do his work to get his teacher off his back. He looked me in the eye saying, "I hate school, it's boring. I can do all that stuff!" Stupid me continued, "You did it all last year, what has changed?" "Really?" He got up and left the room. Oh yeah, everything had changed. Bobby returned at bedtime. I immediately apologized for saying such stupid stuff. He looked at me with a grin saying it wasn't my fault. After all, stupid people say stupid things. We spent the next hour talking about how things had changed. I was surprised how much it bothered him. He described how sometimes he laid in bed late into the night thinking about our family and how he feared the future. I felt closer to Bobby, but I wasn't sure what I could do to help him. (Dad didn't show for the teacher conference. Mom, Bobby, and his teacher worked it out.).

Can't Hide Reality Under a Mask

In mid-October Sue announced at supper that Dad wanted to take Bobby and her out for Halloween in his neighborhood. We looked at Mom. She would call Dad, giving us no indication of whether she was okay with this. Sue pleaded with Mom to let her go. Dad had always been the one to take the kids out while she stayed home giving out candy. Bobby looked at me, shaking his head while mouthing *SB*. Sue's pleading got louder and louder. Mom suddenly raised her voiced yelling, "Enough!" No one said a word through the rest of dinner. When Mom finished eating, she asked Marsha and me to clean up as she headed out the door. This was the first big emotional reaction we'd observed from Mom. She had cried in the past, but nothing like this. Marsha looked at Sue remarking, "Now you did it." Sue rambled on asking why Mom was mad, Dad had always taken her out on Halloween. She was clueless!

Happy Holidays!?!?

The Halloween mess lit the fire under what would become a series of confrontations between them. We had always alternated between both sets of grandparents for Thanksgiving. This year was Mom's family's turn. Dad insisted that we split the day and visit both sets of grandparents. Christmas was a bigger deal. Dad wanted us to spend Christmas Eve at his apartment and Christmas night with his parents. That was a nonstarter for Mom. We had always spent Christmas Eve with her family, Christmas day at home, and Christmas dinner with Dad's family.

Marsha, now in ninth grade, was asked to an overnight New Year's Eve party with several girlfriends. Mom knew their parents and she had no problem with it. Of course, these were Marsha's "black clothes" girlfriends, and Dad would have nothing to do with it. Poor Marsha was caught in the middle. After a heated argument in the driveway, Mom entered the house and told Marsha she could go to the New Year's Eve overnight. Marsha gave Mom a huge hug. I don't think she noticed the tears forming in Mom's eyes. Easter and spring break, well it didn't get any better, if you get my drift.

Cha Cha Cha Changes.....

Mom and Dad had never argued in front of us since the move out. That all changed after Halloween. I overheard many loud phone conversations. Dad often asked us to get Mom out to the car because "they had to talk." Driveway arguments got so loud that we could hear them inside. I wondered what the neighbors thought. Mom was usually in a crappy mood after a battle with Dad. She snapped at us for little things that had never been a big deal in the past. After Christmas she told Dad he could no longer expect to use the van to cart us around. He needed to find a bigger car!

By late winter we all knew things had gotten way worse. Even Sue was finally catching on. Visits seemed more forced. Nobody, including Dad, was having much fun. He rarely had anything planned which resulted in DVDs and take-out. Sue started complaining to Mom. Bobby always brought hand-held video games. Marsha rarely came anymore. I kind of felt stuck in the middle. Did I love Dad, not sure. Did I hate him, not sure. Did I love him and hate him.... maybe! Could I do anything to fix this mess? Probably not!

To this day I can still picture the May family room meeting like it happened yesterday. Mom talked about how things had been rough for us. She had stopped loving Dad long before he left. That was the first time she had admitted not loving him. Thinking back, I don't think I ever heard Mom or Dad say, "I love you." It was like a million little things just added up over time. She wanted out. She wanted to be happy again. That was okay with me, let's just get it over with.

Mom told us she had contacted her lawyer to file for a divorce. Marsha predicted it the night they announced Dad's moving out. Bobby looked at me, half grinned, but did not say SB. Even Sue sat quietly. There were no tears, no running from the room or slamming doors, no losing oneself in a world of video games. We spent the next hour calmly talking about the coming changes. Relief might have been the best word to describe how I felt.

I went to bed that night feeling bad for Mom. I never realized she'd been so unhappy for such a long time before Dad moved. She deserved an Academy Award for playing the "happy mom." She had been our anchor since he left. She tried to keep things going the best she could. Mom was emotionally and physically drained. I think we all were.

Help!

First chance I got, I called Nick. We got together in his basement TV room. I laid it all on the table, my anger, frustration, confusion, feelings of helplessness, you name it! Nick headed upstairs, returning with two large pieces of cardboard, a magic marker, and a nerf football. I sat in silence as he drew a stick man figure on one, labeled Dad, and a woman stick figure on the other, labeled Mom. Nick leaned them against a wall. He flipped me the football saying "enjoy." At first. I wasn't sure what to do. He repeated one of the negative things I had said about my dad and pointed towards the dad figure. I hesitated as he blurted out, "Throw the damn football!" I flipped it at the dad poster. Nick didn't hold back. He picked up the nerf football and wailed it at the dad poster. You can imagine where things went from there. Good thing it was a nerf football. Being a Saturday, Nick suggested I sleep over.

Summertime....

Dad was served divorce papers in late June. Everything had gone downhill since late fall. Dad had started making nasty comments about Mom in front of us. Once Sue asked why he called Mom names. How do you answer that one? He didn't! This divorce thing was theirs, not ours. Dad hadn't come in the house in ages. He often asked me to give Mom messages. I refused and he got mad. Thankfully, Mom never asked me to tell him anything.

Of the kids, I felt worse for Bobby. He had always been somewhat of a loner. He wasn't into athletics and didn't do much with friends outside of school, only on-line. He rarely missed a dad visit. Bobby wasn't negative; however, he rarely got into whatever we did with Dad. Sue's enthusiasm for seeing Dad had lessened by spring. I think the reality of our parent's failed marriage finally hit home. The summer before sophomore year brought about changes in Marsha. I don't know what happened with her "black clothes friends," but one Sunday she came down for breakfast dressed like the old Marsha. The clothes, make-up, jewelry, everything was gone. Nobody said a thing. As she walked to the fridge, Bobby turned to me, grinned, and gave a thumbs up. That summer, Marsha's old friends started showing up.

Summer was tough for Mom. She continued to work full-time while trying to keep the family going. Both Marsha and I picked up more daily household chores and watched Sue. From what I could tell, the divorce filing only made things worse between them. Mom and her friend Clair spent many evenings out on the deck. I didn't try to listen, but occasionally I overheard them talking about money. I was old enough to realize there might be some big changes coming.

Enough Already!

So, it's back to where I started. It's the beginning of eighth grade. Mom filed for divorce several months ago. The divorce seems to be at a standstill. Mom talks to her lawyer, who then talks to Dad's lawyer. I have no idea what's the holdup. Maybe Dad doesn't want a divorce. Maybe he's holding out just to get back at Mom. Doesn't he realize that getting back at Mom also hurts his kids? I try my best to stay out of it. Lately Dad's canceled many visits at the last minute. I don't think any of us cared. Every once in a while, I think back to something Bobby said back in the beginning of this whole mess, "Welcome to the new normal."

Nina

My name is Nina. It's the end of my eighth-grade year. I just turned fourteen, and I live with my mom, but that's not how it's always been. As a little kid, Mom and I lived in an apartment building up several flights of stairs. My grandparents lived a short walk away.

A Little History

Mom worked at a convenient store down the block. Usually, she worked days, but sometimes she worked evenings and got home late at night. I went to preschool several blocks from our place three mornings a week. When she worked, I was shuffled back and forth between Grandma and an older neighbor who we called Aunt Jane. (It wasn't till I was around the third grade that I realized that she really wasn't my aunt.) Grandma worked part-time at her church and thought I was her little angel. There was never a shortage of yummy things to eat. If I wanted to go to the playground, she took me. If I wanted to have a tea party, she became my guest. Grandpa hung a tire swing from the tree in the backyard. He worked during the day and often fell asleep on his lounger after dinner. Grandma said he was tired after his day at work.

First Friend

Aunt Jane was a retired lady who watched several other kids around my age. She wasn't exactly Grandma, but it was good to have other kids to play with. Usually there were two boys and two other girls. A girl named Karen quickly became my friend. Because her parents both worked, she was at Aunt Jane's almost every day. One day, she asked if I could come to her house for a Saturday play date. I had met her parents, and they both seemed really nice. I was very excited. I couldn't wait to get home to tell my mom. I had a real friend, and I was going to her house.

At last the big day arrived. To this day I can remember my first trip to Karen's. Her mom picked me up to take me back to their house. Did I say house? Yes, a house, not an apartment. I'd never been in such a big place. They had a huge backyard with a playhouse, sand box, and swing set. Her room was way bigger than mine, and there was a huge TV room in the basement which was filled with her toys. Her basement didn't look anything like the basement at Grandma's. It didn't look like a basement at all. She even had a TV in her bedroom.

We had a great time. When suppertime came around, she begged her mother to call my mom to see if I could stay. They ordered pizza which a man brought to the front door. I had never seen that happen before. When we had pizza, Mom just took it out of the freezer. It was one of the best days of my life.

After several visits Mom asked if I would like to have Karen over to our place. I always made up some reason why Karen couldn't make it. I think I was just embarrassed by our place. We didn't have a yard. My toys didn't compare, and we only had one TV. I just didn't think we'd have any fun at our apartment.

Kindergarten

Karen was busy that summer before kindergarten with camps and vacations, so I didn't see her very often. Mom took me to Walmart to buy a new outfit for the first day of school. We stopped at McDonalds for lunch on the way home. What could be better!

The first day of kindergarten finally arrived. I looked everywhere for Karen, asking the teacher why she wasn't in my class. I didn't know her last name, she was always just Karen. She said Karen was probably in one of the other kindergarten classes. I would be able to see her at recess and lunch. Recess and lunch came and went, no Karen. After several days, I realized she didn't go to my school.

I begged Mom to call Karen's mom. Karen attended St. Al's, a Catholic school. I remember asking Mom what a Catholic school was and why I couldn't go there with Karen. Mom just smiled. I didn't understand. Karen and I had several more play dates, but things had changed. St. Al's and her new girl-friends were all she talked about. By Christmas our play dates had ended.

Looking back, I think I always realized there were big differences between Karen's family and mine. She had a dad who called her "Lollipop." Her family was always going fun places. I didn't really understand what a vacation was. Her house was big with lots of toys. I'd always been happy, but I began to wonder why she had so much more than me. I just didn't understand, so I asked Mom who laughed, saying cashiers don't make enough money to buy all the nice things Karen's family had. Why didn't Mom get a different job? She just grinned saying Karen's mom and dad both had good jobs. Two workers, two good jobs, lots more money. Why didn't Mom get a "good job?" This might have been the first time I ever wondered why we didn't have a dad around. Two workers, more money and more stuff like Karen? What was wrong with that?

Waking Up / Things Change

Sometime after Christmas, I noticed something different about Mom. Occasionally, she didn't come right home after work. Mom's whole mood seemed to change. She was happier. Mom even started going out on weekend nights. She was fixing her hair, putting on makeup, and sometimes she even wore a dress. She said she was going out with a friend. That was fine with me. I enjoyed being with my grandparents. Friends had never been mentioned before, so this seemed like a good thing. She was happier.

148

One Sunday morning, I woke up at my grandparent's. I wandered downstairs to find them in the kitchen. I asked why I stayed the night. I had fallen asleep at their house many times before, and Mom always came by and took me home. They glanced back and forth and quickly suggested I needed a big bowl of Captain Crunch to start my day. I wasn't really hungry, I was ready to go home. Grandma called to see if Mom was home. Now I was really puzzled. Why wouldn't she be home? It was Sunday morning, so I knew she didn't have to work.

Around lunchtime Mom stopped by to pick me up. I had questions. How come she left me at my grandparents? Was she sick? Did she have a sleep over with her friend? Who was her friend? How come I never got to meet her friend? After all, she had been going out with her more and more for the last several months. From the look on her face, I don't think she liked my questions.

I started spending more weekend nights at my grandparents. I stopped asking questions because it was clear Mom wasn't going to give me straight answers. I just couldn't figure out why Mom was so secretive. Did she like her new friend more than me? I asked Grandma several times about Mom's new girlfriend. Grandma just smiled saying Mom was so busy at work that she needed some fun with her friend. The more questions I asked Grandma, the more she wanted to do things like bake cookies or play a game.

One Sunday morning I came down and could hear my grandparents talking about Mom, so I listened from the hall. Grandpa was not very happy with Mom or Grandma. It was time to quit playing games and introduce me to Jamie. Hmmm, Jamie, well, at least now I had the name of her mystery friend. I had a girl in my kindergarten class named Jamie. I liked her. I hoped I'd like Mom's Jamie. Finally, I couldn't take anymore so I entered the kitchen. They became all smiles, asking if I was hungry. I asked what they were talking about, and they said "nothing" in unison.

I was sitting on my bed playing with my dolls when Mom cautiously entered, sitting next to me. What was up? Mom looked me straight in the eye and said she would like me to meet her friend Jamie. At last, I thought, as I broke into a big smile. When she saw I was happy, the serious look melted from her face. There were a million questions on my mind, but I didn't ask them, keeping secret the conversation I'd overheard between my grandparents. We would meet Jamie at Pizza Hut on Saturday for dinner. After Mom left, I began to wonder what she was like. Mom had been so much more fun lately. Was Jamie the reason she was happier?

Saturday night arrived, and we headed to Pizza Hut. I was both nervous and excited as we took a seat waiting for Jamie's arrival. Mom sat across from me facing the door. Suddenly, she got a nervous smile. A man with an equally nervous smile was approaching. Who was this? The only Jamie I knew was a girl from my kindergarten class. Mom introduced him as he reached across the table to shake my hand.

Memories of dinner are a bit cloudy. He sat next to Mom and asked questions about kindergarten, what I liked to do during the summer, who were my friends, and on and on. Who was this man? Why was he so interested in everything about me? Mom sat by with an uneasy look on her face, occasionally jumping in to answer questions. I was grateful when the pizza arrived. Grandma had taught me it wasn't polite to talk with food in your mouth. I ate slowly!

Neither of us said much on the ride home. I had no clue that Mom had been going out with a guy all these months. My head was spinning. I wasn't sure what I was feeling. I'd never seen Mom with a guy before.

I went off to my room without saying a word where I jumped into bed, curling up with my favorite stuffed animal. Mom came in and sat on my bed as she slowly stroked my hair. I eventually rolled over to face her. She was sorry she hadn't told me about dating Jamie, but she feared I wouldn't like him. I remember crying while asking why she needed to go out with a guy. Weren't me, Grandma and Grandpa enough! We would always be enough, we were family, but sometimes she got lonely, needing somebody to hang out with who was her own age. I wanted to know where she met Jamie. He had been a long-time customer at her store who she had spoken to for years. Several months ago, he had asked her out for coffee after her shift. Okay, finally a few answers, but it didn't really make me feel any better.

The Question

When Mom worked evening shifts during the summer, we often went to the community swimming pool. One day as we ate lunch, I turned to Mom and asked about my dad. I really hadn't planned on asking her. It just sort of came out. I caught her totally off guard. She hesitated at first and then looked off in the distance for a minute before looking back at me. I got really nervous, wondering why I asked such a dumb question. Taking my hands in hers, she started the story.

Mom hadn't dated much in high school, which surprised me because I thought she was the prettiest mom ever. During her senior year Tommy, who graduated the year before, started hanging around her group of friends. Within no time they had become an item. Handsome was the way she described her first boyfriend. He was a painter and was off evenings and weekends. By the end of her senior year, they were inseparable.

Mom enrolled at State College where she planned to study nursing. By August after graduation, she was pregnant. I didn't understand this at all. How could she have a baby? She hadn't said anything about getting married to Tommy. I kept my mouth shut. After being told she was pregnant, Tommy stopped calling. By October he enlisted in the army.

Mom started classes at State College that fall. She dreamed of being a nurse. Being pregnant and working part-time job as a cashier made school impossible. She quit State College after first term, never to return. We lived with my grandparents till I was around two. She worked full-time when we moved into our own apartment.

I remember being really curious about what became of Tommy. She really didn't know. Mom wrote for several months after he left for the army but never got a return letter. Several visits to his parent's house didn't help as she was ignored. She soon realized he was history. I looked at her for a long time in silence. Did she love Tommy? After a brief pause, she teared up and said that she loved me, and that was all that mattered. Mom seemed a little distant the rest of the day. She really didn't seem to be enjoying herself. As I played with other kids in the pool, I noticed her staring into space.

That night I went to bed with all sorts of thoughts dancing through my head. Did Mom ever love Tommy? Did Tommy ever love Mom? I wonder if he knew he had a daughter. If so, did he ever think about me? Why didn't Tommy ever try to contact me? I mean Mom said he was my dad, although, like I said, I really didn't understand where babies came from back then. I wondered if Mom ever missed him. What would it have been like with a dad around all these years? Did Mom still want to be a nurse? In time I drifted off to sleep. I woke up feeling lost and confused. The whole dad thing was still on my mind.

Back To Jamie

Over the summer the three of us went to the park, movies, shopping and out to eat. Mom was in a good mood when Jamie was around. I spent most Saturday nights with my grandparents while they went out. Every once in a while, they'd show up together around noon to pick me up. Why was he with Mom again on Sunday morning when they had just gone out the night before?

On Saturdays I usually watched TV before Mom got up. One Saturday her bedroom door opened and out walked Jamie. I remember his hair was a mess and he was only wearing a pair of pants as he headed to the bathroom. I stared at the bathroom door. What was he doing here? He wasn't here when I went to bed last night. Coming out of the bathroom, he said good morning and headed back into Mom's room. Trying to focus on the TV was useless. What was going on? A little while later, they came out and headed to the kitchen asking if I had eaten yet. I joined them for breakfast. Mom walked to his car with him. Lots of questions.

I was nervous as I asked why Jamie stayed the night. He had stopped over after I was already asleep. It was just easier for him to spend the night. Hmmm ... okay, but was it just like a sleep over, like the kind I had at Karen's? Did they stay up late, watched videos and eat popcorn? Mom just smiled. A smile isn't an answer. I didn't get it.

More nights were being spent at our place. I noticed he left clothes in Mom's room and some of his things showed up in our laundry. A third cup was in our bathroom with a toothbrush and a razor. Mom was less rushed and not as exhausted. He helped with things like the dishes and even cooking. I liked him the more I got to know him. Occasionally we even did things without Mom if she was busy.

One Sunday Mom asked if I would like to see where Jamie lived. It was an actual house, with a driveway, garage and a backyard. The house had a big living room with a huge TV. The kitchen was a separate room that was big enough for a table and chairs. We ate at a counter in our apartment. There was one bedroom on the first floor and two upstairs. It had two bathrooms! It was a lot like my grandparent's home.

Soon we were spending more time at Jamie's than our apartment. One Saturday when we were outside, I saw one of my classmates across the street. Mom took me over to say hi. Carrie was as surprised to see me as I was to see her. Our moms spoke and it was decided that I would spend the afternoon at Carrie's. We continued to spend lots of time together when we were at Jamie's. Spending time at his house was looking better all the time.

Moving

On New Year's Day, Mom looked all serious as we sat on our couch. She asked if I liked Jamie. Of course. What would I think about moving into his house? Really! I didn't know what to say. I had grown to like Jamie over the last few months, and Mom appeared much happier, but the thought of moving in with Jamie never entered my mind. Mom looked worried. I was unsure, kind of scared of what to say. Finally, I said, "Sure, it would be fun." I prayed my answer was the right one. Mom's face instantly relaxed as she broke into a big smile. She reached over and hugged me. My mind was in a jumble as I laid in bed that night. The idea of being across the street from Carrie was exciting. The thought of having Jamie around full-time, not so sure.

The next several weeks went by in a flash. We spent evenings and weekends sorting and packing. Mom's mood continuously changed. One minute, she was yelling at me and Jamie, the next she'd be talking about how much we were going to love his house. Jamie painted my room my favorite color, purple. I got a double bed in a much larger room. As moving day crept closer, I began to feel that maybe this move was a great thing.

Moving day arrived. Mom came to wake me around 7:30. I was already up and dressed. Several of Jamie's friends arrived by 8:00 with a truck. I tried to stay out of their way holding my favorite stuffed pig. By lunchtime, everything we wanted was at Jamie's, or should I say, "our house." Our house, hmmm, I guess that meant the three of us.

The next month was a little crazy as we tried to adjust to our new life together. I was alone with Jamie when Mom had an evening or weekend shift. Spending time alone with Jamie was a little weird. He pretty much left me on my own to entertain myself. Initially he offered to help with homework, but he wasn't very good at it, and we both knew it. I stopped asking for help and he appeared relieved. He spent time working in the garage or sitting in front of the TV drinking beer. I began to miss my grandparents whom I didn't see very often anymore.

My friendship with Carrie blossomed. Her mother didn't mind having me over after school and on weekends. Carrie had lots of neat stuff, so we spent more time at her house than mine. I loved my room, having a backyard, and having a friend across the street.

Leaping Ahead

The end of fourth grade was approaching. Mom looked into enrolling in a two-year x-ray technician program at the community college. She was nervous and excited, Jamie, not so much. She continued to work part-time at the store. Her free time was taken up with school. Although I didn't see her as much, that was okay. I was older and didn't mind spending more time on my own, and Carrie and I were together most days anyways. At first, Mom was afraid of going back to school because of her age, but within weeks, she grew in confidence. She loved it!

Early in fifth grade, I noticed something going on between Mom and Jamie. He complained she was never around and was always busy with school when she was home. Arguments occurred more often. Frequently Jamie went out after dinner or came home late after work. School and work kept Mom so busy that I'm not sure she cared what he was doing. Being home became less fun. I noticed a lot more beer bottles when I took out the recycling.

Not So Holly Jolly

Mom prepared a big breakfast Christmas morning. She acted happy and I hoped things were finally better between them. Jamie came from the bedroom looking terrible. His hair was a mess, his breath smelled, and he reeked of body odor. Mom tried to put on a "Merry Christmas" face. I could see her disappointment as he refused any breakfast and took a cup of coffee to the living room, turning on the TV. After breakfast, we joined him to exchange gifts. It was not a holly jolly time.

Jamie said he'd drive himself as we left for my grandparents for Christmas dinner. Grandpa got madder as we delayed dinner for him. Finally, Grandma suggested we eat. Mom went out on the porch to make a call, returning to say Jamie was not feeling well. After dinner we exchanged presents. It was fun, but it wasn't. Mom seemed to be faking it, Grandma made a bigger fuss than normal, and Grandpa grumbled to himself.

Mom and Grandma went to the kitchen to clean up while Grandpa looked for a Christmas movie. On my way to the bathroom, I heard Mom crying as she spoke with Grandma. I couldn't understand much of what they were saying, however, I heard Jamie's name several times. They both looked upset when they came back to watch the movie. Everybody was pretty quiet the rest of the evening. It was like we all wanted to say something, but no one dared.

Neither of us spoke on the short ride home. We entered an empty house. I guess Jamie wasn't sick. As Mom turned to me, her eyes filled with tears. I quickly darted up to my room. About a half hour later, she knocked on my door, staring at the floor as she entered. I could barely hear as she apologized for such a bad Christmas. I scooted close and told her it wasn't her fault. We talked about how things had changed between them. She believed their troubles started when she went back to school. Mom looked sad as she talked about how useless she felt as a store cashier, but a smile returned when talking about her x-ray tech program. Younger classmates looked up to her. Mom felt important!

The Morning After

I woke up the next morning to yelling and screaming. Jamie got home late Christmas night and was drunk. I put my head under my pillow. I couldn't stand to hear it. I tried to hold back the tears, but it didn't work. Eventually things quieted down after the front door banged shut, so I slowly went downstairs to find Mom on the couch hugging her knees and crying. Did Jamie hit her? Tears poured down her face as she shook her head no. Not knowing what to do, I turned and ran back to my room where I spent the rest of the morning waiting for her to knock on my door, but it never happened. At lunch, Mom said "they'd work it out, don't worry." Right, I worried. I felt very lonely in my purple room as I waited to go to my grandparents since she worked evening shift. Were Mom and Jamie splitting up?

At my grandparents, I tried to act happy, but I didn't do too good a job. After dinner, Grandma sat next to me on the couch and put her arm around me. I cried. Thank God, no questions.

The Next Several Months

Jamie was around less, and there was a strange silence when he was. I began to hate being at home, so I went to Carrie's or my grandparent's whenever I had the chance. I told Carrie everything. Nothing at our house was the same anymore. I knew Mom was really busy, but I missed her so much. Looking back, I think she was as unhappy as I had become. I felt so alone on evenings and weekends. I'm sure Carrie's mom suspected something. She often baked treats and took us to fun places to cheer me up. I began to hate it when I couldn't go over to their house.

One night when I got up to use the bathroom, I heard a noise down downstairs. I could see Mom sleeping on the couch. I wasn't sure what to think. The next day I told her I'd seen her on the couch. She and Jamie were not getting along, and she did not want to share his bed right now. Hmmm ... It seemed like I wasn't the only person who was feeling lonely these days. Frequent memories about our life before Jamie filled my head. Why did we ever move in with him? We were doing fine before Jamie, weren't we? He had become a jerk! I was beginning to hate him. Nothing good was happening at home anymore! No one was happy!

Summertime Blues

Mom finished classes in May and had two weeks off before summer term. She was on the phone a lot and ran many errands. What was up? By now Jamie was rarely around and the three of us never did anything together. He hung in the garage and usually smelled like beer. I continued to get out of the house every chance I had.

Mom and I went out to dinner after my last day of school. As dessert arrived, she got that serious look on her face. We'd be moving in several weeks. Where were we moving to? Did we have a house or were we going back to our apartment? Was I still going to the same school next year? Did my grandparents know? What were we going to do for furniture, since we had given most of our things away? Would I still see Carrie?

For a short while we would move in with my grandparents. Because Mom was only working part-time, there wasn't enough money for our own place. When she finished school, she would be making much more money as an x-ray tech, and we'd get our own place. She took the guest bedroom, and I took over Grandma's craft room. My grandparents were pleased. They took me to visit Carrie and she came over often. Mom slowly returned to her old self and I began to feel much better. It's been tough seeing Mom so unhappy the last few months at Jamie's. I hoped we'd never see him again!

New Beginnings

Mom graduated in May and took a job at St. Francis Hospital. We planned to stay with my grandparents a while longer so she could save money for our own place. A little while turned out to be a year, but nobody seemed to mind. Happiness had returned!

Mom loved her job and the people she worked with. Occasionally she went out with co-workers and we went to hospital family events. When it was time to find our own place, my only request was not to change schools. A small two-bedroom house close to my grandparents and school was available to rent. Grandpa had retired so he helped with painting and fixing little things. I was within walking distance of everything I needed. What more could I ask for?

After Fourteen Years ... Really!!!

I'll never forget the date, Friday September 17th. I came straight home from school and was laying on my bed listening to tunes when the doorbell rang. I had no idea who the middle-aged guy was on our porch, so I didn't answer it. I guess, he saw the curtain move so he called my name. That freaked me out. Who was this guy? I yelled that my mom would be home in minutes. He yelled he knew her, and he just wanted to introduce himself. I ran to the back door to make sure it was locked and called Mom. She didn't pick up, so I left a voice message. He had not left, so I called my grandparents. By the time they arrived he was gone.

We were in the living room when Mom got home. She asked me to describe the man. He was around her age, a little taller than Mom, with dark hair and a moustache. He wasn't fat or anything. He just kind of looked like a normal guy. They exchanged glances. What was going on? They said nothing, telling me not to worry. I didn't believe them for a minute. That look on their faces I'd seen before. It wasn't an "everything is peachy" look. How did he know my name? Again, they exchanged worried glances saying they didn't know. Grandma suggested we go out to dinner. She talked constantly, trying to forget the porch guy. Mom's mind seemed elsewhere. What was going on? I was positive they all knew something about the man on the porch. I had trouble getting to sleep that night. The whole thing was more than a little bit scary. I hadn't felt this way since we move out of Jamie's.

One evening, Mom got a call from an unknown caller, which she let go to voice mail. She went to her room to listen to it. She came out looking upset, as she sat next to me. Oh boy, that look again. Mom's and my grandparent's suspicions about the guy on the porch were confirmed by the voice mail. My real dad was the guy on the porch. In Mom's eyes, Tommy was past history. She had no idea why he showed up now. Anxiety and fear increased as I laid awake in bed for hours that night. Things had been going so good. Why did he have to show up? Did he think he could get back with Mom? The look on her face and the tone of her voice made me think that this whole thing was freaking her out as much as it had me. God, now what? We'd finally gotten back to where everybody was happy.

Mom wasn't herself the next several weeks. I suspected it had to do with Tommy's appearance. Nothing around the house was right. Sometimes I'd be talking to her, but it was like she was in another world. Alone, lost, confused, worried, scared, were all feelings I experienced. I was uneasy about staying home by myself, so I started going to my grandparents after school until she got home from work.

I admit, I was curious about Tommy, but fourteen years, why show up now? Did he want to see Mom, me, or both of us? Why didn't he contact Mom before showing up on the porch? Did he really think a teenage girl would open the door to a stranger? He must think I'm an idiot! How did he know where we lived? Why, why, why was this all happening? Too many questions, no answers! My emotions were all over the place.

At first, I didn't want to tell anyone what happened. The idea of my dad, a total stranger trying to wedge his way back into my life was scary. Finally, I told Carrie. She said I'd been acting differently lately but was afraid to ask. Carrie didn't judge and didn't ask questions. She just listened. As I started to cry, she started to cry. We hugged. At least I had gotten it out. I felt better, even though I had no idea what was going to happen next.

Mom came to my room one afternoon with that look on her face. Here we go again. Looking me straight in the eye, she asked if I wanted to meet Tommy. I didn't know what to say. I was mad! Why did he abandon us? We'd been through some rough times. Mom gave up her dream of becoming a nurse. What would we have done without help from my grandparents? Still, another side of me was curious about him. The decision was totally mine. I wanted some time to think about it.

I called Carrie hoping she'd tell me what to do. She didn't. I knew the decision was mine. The next day after school, Grandma sensed something was bugging me. We drank lemonade in silence for several minutes, then I cried. We talked and talked. We didn't just speak about the "big decision," but about all sorts of things Mom and I had been through. By the time I left, I'd made up my mind. For better or worse, I was going to meet Tommy.

That night I told Mom my decision. I couldn't tell if she was pleased, relieved, unhappy, or what. She would contact him to work things out. My only request was that I do it alone. I didn't want their history to get in the way. That was fine, but she said it would have to be in a public place like a restaurant. That worked for me.

Pizza Hut … Again?

The following Saturday Mom took me to Pizza Hut. Are you kidding, that's where I met Jamie, and we all know how well that ended! I kept my mouth shut. I repeatedly asked myself,

"Why am I doing this?" I hadn't slept much Friday. My stomach was in a knot as we got out of the car. I just wanted to get it over.

We spotted Tommy already seated in a booth. Mom would be in the parking lot if I felt uncomfortable and wanted to leave. They both appeared uneasy as I was introduced. This was the first time they'd seen each other since he left for the army. Tommy offered to drive me home. Thank God Mom said no!

Awkward would be an understatement. At first, we sat in silence, then Tommy started by asking how I was. What could I say, I didn't know how I was! One part of me wanted to get out of there. Another part wanted to see where this was headed. I could see he was nervous. I experienced a little guilty pleasure watching him squirm. After a few minutes of know nothing questions, Tommy paused, looked down at the table, and started to apologize for leaving pregnant Mom all alone. This caught me by surprise, an apology, really? What did he want me to do? I should maybe say, no big deal. Welcome back into my life! Asshole! Should I forgive somebody I didn't even know? I was just pissed off. The nerve of this guy!

The last couple of weeks had been a mess. Mom was not herself. My grandparents were acting different. My emotions were scattered. He went on about how he really liked my mom, but never thought they'd get married. Thinking back, I realize he never used the word "love" when talking about Mom. He had freaked out when told she was pregnant. What was he thinking? Hadn't he heard of condoms? Lucky for him, the waitress came to take our order. When she left, we sat in silence again. All the questions I rehearsed vanished. Tommy returned to questions about my life, blah, blah, blah, nothing too deep. The waitress saved me again with our food.

After we finished eating, I asked my first and only question. Where have you been for the last fourteen years? Tommy paused before starting. He had been in the army for two years where he learned how to work on vehicles. After the army, he found a job in a garage on the other side of town. He met someone and got married. Tommy smiled when he talked about his two daughters. His mood changed when he said they divorced. I got uncomfortable as Tommy sadly talked about only seeing his daughters once a week. Tommy nodded in the direction of the door. I turned to see my mom walking towards us. I was relieved. When we stood, he asked when we could get together again. I quickly looked at Mom. She took my hand, said bye, and we headed to the door. The last thing Tommy said was "I'll call."

Luckily Mom didn't play twenty questions on the drive home, only asking once if I was okay. I stared out the car window and she left it at that. I called Carrie when I got to my room. I didn't know what I wanted to tell her. I just needed to hear her voice. Gradually I filled her in. Several times, she referred to Tommy as "your dad." That felt weird. I hadn't thought of him that way. He was just Tommy. When we hung up, the "dad" thing stuck in my head. He'd never been a dad to me. I was fourteen and I just met him. No, the "dad" title wasn't going to work.

At dinner, I could tell Mom was still uneasy about my lunch with Tommy, but she was cool and didn't force the issue. Later that evening, I broke down while watching TV. Mom joined me on the couch and the flood gates opened. We talked forever about the last fourteen years. She had looked into Tommy's background and knew that he lived in town, had been married and had two girls. She had to make sure I would be safe before she agreed to let me meet him. I asked if I had to see him again. She said it was up to me. That's not what I wanted to hear. I wanted Mom to say "no!"

Again?

Things got back to normal over the next several weeks. Then one Saturday, who shows up on the porch around dinner time, Tommy. I answered the door but did not let him in. I was so glad Mom was home. She went out on the porch. The conversation got hot. I overheard Tommy say things like: "She's my daughter too. You have no right to keep her from me. Don't you think she wants to see her dad?" Mom screamed, "How dare you come over here after you've been drinking. Fourteen years, fourteen years, what do you expect?" I called my grandparents. As they pulled up, he stormed off the porch. Mom was really calm when she came back inside. Grandpa was furious and wanted to call the police, but she talked him out of it. Grandma was unusually quiet.

After they left, we talked. Tommy had called her several times over the last several weeks. Obviously, she had not told me.

Was she trying to protect me or herself? I guess seeing Tommy after all those years had upset her more than I realized. I wasn't angry with Mom, I just felt bad for her. Mom, my grandparents and I were in a good place. The return of Tommy messed up everything. She shared that Tommy had been a drinker years ago. His behavior today only convinced her he had not changed. She now worried about my safety if I was alone with him. I'd made up my mind, I never wanted to see him again.

I went to bed that night with emotions going in a million directions. Tommy's behavior on the porch and Mom's description of him from years ago frightened me. My grandparent's reaction made me wonder if they knew more about him than they would ever share. If he was wild when he dated Mom, did that mean that she was wild? Did she get pregnant because she and Tommy were drunk? I don't think I wanted to know. Falling asleep started to become a nightly problem. Too much going on in my head! I just kept rewinding the events of the last several weeks.

Over the next month, life settled down again. Mom told me he called three times, demanding to see me. The conversations were short, with Mom telling him it was not going to happen. I was in the other room during one of the conversations and was proud of the way she kept her cool, remaining stern but polite. The situation was over and I tried to bury my curiosities about Mom's sperm donor.

The Call Restarted It All

We had an in-service day about two months after the second porch scene. I was expecting a call from Joann for a ride to basketball practice. I answered my cell on the first ring. Guess who? You got it, Tommy. He knew I was off school and would be over soon. I was shocked. How did he get my cell number? I hung up and called Mom, but it went to voice mail. I texted her. I called Grandma and Grandpa but got no answer. I got more nervous by the minute. What if he came over? I wasn't going to let him in the house. My phone rang again, but this time I looked at the screen and saw it was Joann. I quickly told her what had happened, and they arrived within minutes and took me back to their place.

Mom called shortly after I got to Joann's. She listened silently as I told her what occurred. She wanted to leave work, but I insisted she pick me up at the gym after practice. My grandparents were already coming over for dinner. That evening the four of us talked about what to do. Grandpa wanted Mom to go to court and get a restraining order against Tommy. Mom first wanted to try to handle it with a phone call. Grandma kept repeating everything would be okay. I wasn't so sure. How did he know I was off school and what about my phone number? Only family and a few friends had it. Mom had told him he was not welcome, yet he called. Was he stupid or what? I was to have a ride to and from school and practices unless I had two friends with me. Mom would try to set him straight! I only hoped.

I was outside the door listening when Mom called Tommy. She repeatedly told him that he was not to contact the two of us again, slowly getting madder as the call dragged on. Suddenly, it was like a dam broke. "Why did you run away all those years ago? You were man enough to get me pregnant but not man enough to own up to it? I actually thought we were in love. Big tough guy runs away by joining the army. You couldn't even contact me when you got out. Why now, why now! Do you have any idea what we went through? I quit college and worked at a crappy convenient store. If it wasn't for my parents, I don't know what would have happened. Think about that Tommy. What might Nina's life have been like? Then you show up all these years later. You knew I wasn't home. You always were a coward. And then you show up a second time after you'd been drinking! You're crazy if you think I'm going to let Nina ever go with you." With that, the phone call ended. I quickly headed back to the living room acting like I was watching something on my phone. Within minutes Mom joined me. She turned to me and asked if I enjoyed the conversation. She knew that I knew. Years of hidden emotions spilled out.

What's Next?

The next several weeks were more than a little tense. We all prayed Tommy would stay away, but we weren't convinced he would. And sure enough, he didn't. It happened one evening at my basketball game. As I walked back to the bench during a time out, I spotted him sitting in the top row of the bleachers. I immediately looked in the direction of my family. I'm sure they didn't know he was there. The game resumed and my play went right down the toilet. I was completely distracted. At one point, I made eye contact with Tommy who broke into a big smile. I wanted to throw up.

At half-time coach asked if I was feeling okay. I felt sick and he sat me the rest of the game. Thankfully, Tommy was seated behind our bench, so I could easily avoid looking at him. When the game was over, I quickly headed to my family. They knew something was wrong since I usually played most of the game. We were almost to the car when Tommy yelled out, "Hey Nina, aren't you going to say hi to your dad?" Everyone turned in a flash. He was headed our way. Mom told Grandma to get me in the car. Tommy was all smiles. Mom was furious as she asked him what he was doing. He said he just wanted to see his daughter. Mom said he had given up those rights years ago and got in the car. Grandpa just stood there, arms crossed, staring at him while shaking his head. I think we were afraid Grandpa might hit him. Was this ever going to end?

No one said much of anything as we ate pizza back at our place. Even Grandma didn't have anything to say. As we sat in the living room after dinner, Mom admitted that this had gone on too long, and she was going to make an appointment with a lawyer. Grandpa smiled, Grandma looked nervous. I didn't know much about lawyers, but I felt relieved. Sleep did not come quickly, but I think it was because I was excited Mom was going get some help to get Tommy out of our lives.

Lawyers

A meeting was scheduled with a lawyer, Ms. Fredricks. Mom was to document everything, starting with his first visit to the porch. None of his phone calls would be answered, but she kept track of dates, times, and saved any voice messages. Ms. Fredricks also wanted my version of what occurred. A registered letter was sent to Tommy requesting that he not contact us. She hoped he would leave us alone after receiving her letter. If he came around again, Mom should consider a restraining order. Ms. Fredricks informed us that Tommy could go to court in an attempt to see me, although she doubted it would come to that. She tried to reassure me that he would probably just go away. I had my doubts. We also agreed that I would get a new phone number and continue to be with two friends if I was out in the neighborhood.

Ms. Fredricks was wrong, I was right. Tommy was an idiot! He called every several days for weeks. Records were kept and all voice messages were sent to Ms. Fredricks. Most voice messages didn't make much sense. Mom questioned whether he was drunk. A restraining order was the next step. I felt scared and powerless. Would a restraining order bring the police into this mess? Why had Tommy ever tried to contact us? This was the second time he hurt Mom. It was all so unfair. She never did anything but try to make a good life for us. I just wanted to delete this whole thing from my brain!

A restraining order was issued, phone calls stopped. I was a little surprised. I think he got the message. I hope he got the message. Thank God!

What Might Have Been

My eighth-grade year came to an end. Life slowly returned to normal. I started sleeping a little better and Mom and my grandparents all seemed a lot less tense. Mom got a promotion, made several close friends from work, and even played in the hospital volleyball league. My grandparents planned a cruise they had talked about for years.

I don't know about myself. Somedays I still feel like I am always looking over my shoulder. Would Tommy show up again? I knew he drank and that increased my anxious fear. I was so pissed at what he had done to Mom all those years ago. I know I should, but I just can't let that anger go! I began to realize how hard it had been for Mom, how much she had sacrificed for me. I'm not sure either of us would have made it without my grandparents.

Sometimes I wonder what it would have been like to have had a dad around all those years. Thank God it wasn't Tommy. What if mom had married a guy who cared for us? She could have become a nurse, and we could have done more family things, like vacations. Maybe I'd have a brother or sister. There would have been a dad for Dads and Doughnuts at school and Father Daughter dances. Would he have coached one of my teams? I guess I never really thought much about these types of things until recently. Believe me, I'm not complaining, but I can't help but wonder what might have been?

Olivia

My name is Olivia, and I am currently in the tenth grade. I have a sister, Cassie, who is two years older and a brother Sam, who is six. Mom and Dad split up four years ago. I guess every kid thinks their story is unique. I'm no different.

A Little Background

My parents were married about a year after they graduated college. Dad got a job selling insurance. You know auto, home and life. Mom majored in Women's Studies. You can imagine the number of job openings in that field – like none. She bounced around from job to job but never found anything that satisfied her. Mom became pregnant with Cassie after being married for about two years. Dad apparently was a good insurance salesman because he opened his own office when Cassie was around a year old. Mom gave up her job search and became the secretary at Dad's new place, Harbor Insurance.

There was enough space at Harbor for Mom to set up a small nursery and play area, eliminating the need for childcare. To hear Mom tell it, having Cassie around when clients came in helped Dad sell many policies. Harbor Insurance grew quickly. By the time I was born, Dad had employed an additional agent. Mom stayed at home with Cassie and me. Dad hired a new secretary.

About the time I started preschool, we moved into a bigger house with a huge backyard. Mom continued to stay home with us. She went back to work part-time at Harbor Insurance when Cassie and I were both in school full-time. School was great fun. I had friends in our neighborhood, played youth soccer and was a Girl Scout. My grades were always good. I never caused any trouble. I was like the model student.

We went on a week-long vacation to Florida every summer and spent a long weekend at a State Park cabin every winter. Dad usually worked several evenings a week, yet he made it to most of our events. Mom worked a day or two a week and volunteered at our school. Mom became pregnant with Sam when I started fourth grade. Mom stopped working at the office with the arrival of Sam. Dad was fine with that.

Up to that point, I can't say I ever recall any big issues between Mom and Dad. Dad seemed happy at his expanding insurance agency, and Mom seemed happy being a mom. They started what they called "date night" several Saturdays a month. Everything seemed really good. I don't have any bad memories of our family back then. Everyone got along. We were like the perfect TV family!

Yoga

Sometime around the start of fifth grade, Mom joined a yoga class. They had childcare so it was easy to take Sam. At first Mom went one or two times a week, but it quickly progressed to three and even four times. I guess you could say she was "into yoga." I recall Dad saying how good she looked, having lost something he called "baby pounds." Mom quickly developed new lady friends from her yoga class. It wasn't unusual for them to go out for dinner a couple times a month. Dad encouraged her to go out and have a little fun.

One night at dinner in the spring of fifth grade, Mom informed everyone that she had signed up for training to become a Certified Yoga Instructor. Becky, a friend from class, was taking yoga instructor training also. Training started May 1st. I really didn't know much about yoga, but Mom was very excited about becoming an instructor so I thought it must be good, right? Dad seemed especially supportive and proud that she was doing something for herself. Mom was a certified instructor by late fall and soon led a class with Becky.

Winter

As winter progressed, yoga began to occupy more of Mom's time. She took on several evening classes and often went out afterwards. This put a little strain on the family. Mom and Dad juggled their schedules so one of them was home with us. Even though things had changed, everyone adapted. Cassie, being the oldest, was given a few more chores. My memories of that time were good. Dad's growing business was obvious by the new Toyota Highlander he purchased for Mom. She seemed to be enjoying herself.

Even though Mom was very involved with her yoga, she didn't talk about her yoga friends. We knew first names, but that was about it. Once while cleaning up from dinner, Dad asked if she'd like to invite her yoga friends and spouses over for dinner. Mom was quick to turn the idea down. Dad seemed puzzled, maybe even a little hurt, but he didn't push it.

One Sunday night a few weeks after Christmas, I heard Mom and Dad get into their first loud argument. Maybe I should correct myself, it was Dad who got loud, not Mom. Sure, I'd seen them argue before, but this was different. I couldn't make out everything, but it seemed like Dad was fed up with Mom's steadily increasing time spent teaching yoga and hanging out with her yoga friends. He was happy that she had found something she liked, yet he expressed frustration that she had become more lax in keeping up household and family responsibilities. He pointed out he had to work several evenings a week if they wanted to maintain their lifestyle – whatever that meant. He argued that she made next to nothing teaching yoga, but she was spending plenty on yoga outfits and hanging out with friends. He complained that she even missed several of our sporting events and rarely volunteered at school anymore.

What was going on? I thought things were fine, but the big argument made me wonder. They gave each other the cold shoulder all week. Oh, they spoke, but only when necessary. Neither tried to hide their bruised feelings from the kids. Saturday date night didn't happen. I only remember them missing one previous date night when Sam was sick back in October. I'd be lying if I said I wasn't a little worried. I wondered if Cassie was worried too. I desperately wanted to talk to her but was afraid of what she'd say. Would she blow me off? Being a seventh grader, Cassie started to see herself as being pretty important, spending less time with me. Maybe I was just imagining things, blowing the fight up into something it wasn't. Was it all just drama? I saw drama all the time with girls at school. Was this just parent drama? I mean, the girls at school always got over it in a few days, if not a few hours. This had gone on for a week!

The tension between them seemed to lessen a little over the next week. However, one thing didn't change. Mom still went out with her friends after yoga, returning after we were in bed. I tried to put the whole thing out of my mind; however, there was still a nagging feeling that things weren't right. I replayed their argument like a thousand times in my head. I desperately tried not to take sides, yet I found myself agreeing more with Dad. Yoga was okay, but why was she going out so often? Dad never went out with his buddies. He just worked and worked. Dad was tired, yet he tried to help with homework and other family stuff. By the end of week two, I was starting to feel sorry for him. I fought off not getting mad at Mom. What was she doing? We had always been so happy. Not so much the last few weeks. That Saturday they left on date night around at 7:00 returning by 9:00. They usually got home around 11:00. What had happened?

I finally cornered Cassie. She agreed that things seemed a little tense between Mom and Dad; however, she didn't see it as a big deal. She stood up for Mom, saying that she had found something she liked, and Dad should accept and encourage it. Cassie felt Mom must have been really bored staying home all those years watching us kids. Cassie said she was never going to give up her career to be a housewife raising kids. I'd never looked at it that way before. I can't recall Mom ever having a close group of lady friends prior to yoga. I guess she deserved friends.

Cassie also thought that maybe Dad had to back off a little on his work hours. He always bragged how business was good and what a great team he had assembled. So, let the team pick up more of the work. After all, he was the owner. Maybe Cassie was right, things between Mom and Dad were probably fine. Maybe I was letting my imagination get the better of me.

Nothing much changed over the next several months. If they had any more arguments, they didn't happen when I was around. Their schedules remained about the same, with both of them out of the house two evenings a week. We all sort of got used to it. Sam was to the age that he was easy for Cassie and me to watch for short periods. Despite us settling into a routine, something still didn't seem right. Saturday date nights continued, but neither seemed very excited about it. I noticed less affection between Mom and Dad, like – you know

– hugs and kisses. So, things were peaceful, but were they right? On several TV shows, I'd heard couples talk about how they had grown apart. Was this happening with my parents? I was convinced that they didn't hate each other, but did they still love each other? I guess I was just being stupid. Why should I worry about such stuff? The problem was, I found myself thinking about Mom and Dad more and more.

One Sunday evening in April, Dad brought up our summer vacation. Dad worked it out to take two weeks off in a row, so he wanted to go somewhere other than Florida. From the look on Mom's face, I don't think they had discussed it. Dad enthusiastically tried to get our ideas of where to go. Cassie immediately brought up Yellowstone National Park. I had seen TV shows on Yellowstone and quickly agreed. Dad's face broke into a broad smile at the suggestion. I couldn't tell if Mom was excited about Yellowstone or not. Dad immediately jumped up, got the iPad, plopped himself on the couch and invited us to gather around as we looked up information. Cassie, Sam, Dad and I were excited. Mom stood behind the couch hardly saying a thing.

I had trouble getting to sleep, with my imagination going wild over the possibilities of a family vacation to Yellowstone. Unfortunately, being awake allowed me to hear the second major argument between my parents. Obviously, Dad had not discussed any of this vacation stuff with Mom. This time Mom was not quiet during the argument. My excitement over a Yellowstone vacation turned to worry.

Summer / Fall / Winter / Spring / Summer

The vacation to Yellowstone was on. Dad did most of the planning but who cared, as long as we got to go. I can't recall any more big arguments. Date night, once the rule, had become an exception. July 6th came and off we headed to Yellowstone. The drive took forever, but everybody – I mean everybody – had a good time when we got there. Maybe things were back to normal.

There was no real tension in the house the last month of summer vacation. Dad was back at the insurance agency, and Mom was doing her yoga thing. Cassie and I started soccer practice and Sam was growing like a weed.

In early September, Mom announced that she was going away for several days in October with her friends to view the fall leaf changes. Dad remarked about how much fun that would be. No objections, no questioning, just positive encouragement. Wow, things had definitely changed since their big arguments last year.

Becky, Jonnie, and Brianna showed up one Sunday afternoon in October to pick up Mom for their trip. I should mention that by now I had met Becky several times. Dad went out to the car to greet Mom's friends. It was kind of weird. I guess it was good that she was going, but weren't vacations for families? Dad acted okay with it, so I suppose I should have been more okay with it too. Mom came home Thursday evening in a great mood. She gave few details about her trip except that they took hikes and ate at some wonderful restaurants.

Nothing much else happened the remainder of fall and winter. I didn't hear any more arguments through my bedroom walls. Date nights were still rare. Springtime arrived and Mom took another short trip with her yoga friends. Again, Dad seemed fine with it. I was a little jealous that the family didn't go somewhere over spring break.

April arrived and Dad called the entire family together to talk about summer vacation. With at least two weeks off, he thought we should again go somewhere other than Florida. I suggested the Smoky Mountains, Cassie brought up California, and Mom said nothing. Dad, apparently still on the outdoor kick from last year, brought up the Grand Canyon. Well, who wouldn't want to see the Grand Canyon? Afterwards, I realized that Mom was neither positive or negative. She just sat there as we explored our trip options on the iPad. There was no argument that night, as there had been last year.

Our second trip out West was just as much fun as the first trip. In addition to the Grand Canyon, we stopped at the St. Louis Arch on the way out and visited the Great Sand Dunes, Mesa Verde, and Durango in Colorado. Everyone got along. It was great! Our family was back!

Shock Waves

One Thursday in early September, Mom asked the kids to come to the family room. Dad wasn't home. I had no idea what was up. Mom started by saying how much she loved us. Duh, of course, she loved us. She's our mom! What was she saying this for? She talked about how much fun we all had the last two summer vacations. I was getting nervous. Where was this all going? She even stated how important Dad was to her. Looking back years later, I realize, she didn't use the word "love" when talking about Dad. She used the word "important." Really, important? Your job is important, grades are important, getting exercise is important, your husband is way different than important! What was going on? Were they splitting up? No, that couldn't be. Things seemed pretty good for some time. I couldn't even recall a minor fight in ages. Finally, she just said it. She was moving in with her friend Becky.

We sat for – like forever – in total silence. A few tears appeared on Mom's cheek. Sam was the first to speak up, asking point blank. How can you live with Becky and us at the same time? Mom tried to explain that she wasn't going to live with us anymore. She was moving in with Becky. Sam was completely confused as he continued to ask questions. Mom was moving this weekend. She had told Dad several days ago. That explained why he hadn't been around the last few days. Cassie got up and ran out the door. Mom hugged both Sam and me, but I didn't respond. Mom looked me in the eyes as she released her hug. I looked away. I felt like I was drowning. I closed my eyes and all I could see in my head was my mother fading away. When I opened them, she was staring out the window. I stood, took Sam's hand, and left.

We retreated to Sam's bedroom. He didn't stop with the questions. The problem was, I had no answers. The more he asked, the more upset he got. I tried to keep my cool, but I could feel myself melting down. God, this was terrible! I had a hard time paying attention to anything Sam was saying. Mom and Dad were breaking up? Even though I had my concerns in the past, I didn't see this coming. What had gone wrong? The vacations were great but now Dad was just "important" to her? I thought we had all adapted pretty good to the changes around the house since Mom had started with yoga.

Eventually, Sam was all questioned out. He picked up his video game controller which was my cue to leave. The house was dead silent. Dad wasn't home, I had no idea where Mom was, and Cassie hadn't returned. I went to my room and sat on my bed staring out the window. My mind was blank. I was feeling nothing. I didn't know whether to cry, scream, or throw things. I don't know if I ever felt so alone in all my life. I feared that I was going to get sick. Nothing made sense. I'd been to several weddings. What happened to the promise, you know, "for better or worse, richer or poor, in sickness and health?" Becky was Mom's best friend, but why would they move in together? If they had fought more, if Dad had mistreated Mom, at least I'd have an excuse for why she was moving out. I had nothing!

I heard the back door open, and within minutes, Cassie entered our room. For the longest time, we just looked at each other without uttering a word. She had been out walking around the neighborhood. Finally, her anger spilled out. Now she blamed Mom and her yoga friends for the mess. We talked, but got nowhere, just more confused.

Around 9:30 we heard Dad's footsteps on the stairs. It dawned on me that our whole conversation centered around how Mom's moving out was going to screw us. I don't think we ever brought up Dad. Suddenly, I felt worse, I mean, Dad might be losing his wife. If our lives were going to change, his life was probably going to change a lot more. I wanted to run out in the hallway to see him, but I didn't know what I would say. Cassie and I both chickened out and stayed in our room. As I lay in bed that night, one phrase swirled around my brain. "What just happened?"

Off to Becky's

Friday was just weird. At breakfast everyone acted as if nothing had happened the night before. We headed off to school and work like any other day. Friday night, Cassie went to a friend's, Dad stayed late at the office, and Mom was in their room – apparently packing. Sam and I watched TV. I hated it. Why wouldn't anybody say something about Mom moving out the next day. This was not normal! I was not okay! I wanted to scream, but I felt like I had no one to scream to. No one would hear me.

Mom got up early on Saturday to take a carload of clothes to Becky's. I hadn't slept much. I heard her in the hallway as the sun was rising. I wanted to go out and say something, but I didn't. What would I say? Hey, can I help you with those bags? Mom, I hope you like your new house. What's your new room like? I guess Dad won't keep you awake with his snoring anymore. Boy, that must be a relief! Don't worry about us. We'll get along fine without you. Mom, do you and Becky have any vacations planned like our fun family vacations? What does Dad think about this? Are you guys getting a divorce? Oh, you don't have to say anything. I'm sure you'll spring it on us at the last minute, right? It was scary, worrisome, depressing, sad, but most of all, overwhelming. I just didn't get it - any of it!

Mom returned while we ate breakfast. Dad wasn't home. She assured us that she'd see us several times a week. They planned for us to come over to Becky's for dinner next weekend. She had made a copy of our sports schedules and would continue to help Dad getting us to practices and games. She confessed that she had been thinking of moving in with Becky for some time. She realized that this was a major shock to us. Mom wanted us to get to know Becky better. Becky had become very important in her life. I thought to myself. What about Dad and us? Where did we rank? Is Becky now number one in your life? What if I didn't want anything to do with Becky? Becky stole you away from the family. None of us said a thing. Sam kept looking back and forth between Cassie and me. I expected him to break into tears at any moment. Cassie was grinding her teeth while nervously bouncing her foot up and down. My confusion was rapidly turning to anger. Mom said this had nothing to do with us. She loved us as much today as ever. She repeated several times that moving in with Becky was "something she had to do." She encouraged us to call her anytime. Yeah, right! She was the last person on earth I wanted to call.

Dad Returns

When Dad got back, he gathered us in the family room. We'd hardly seen him since Wednesday night. I remember thinking: here we go again, what's he going to tell us? Is he leaving too? Dad said he was as surprised as we were by Mom's move to Becky's. She had told him the previous weekend, with the agreement that she would be the one to tell us. He apologized for not being around for the last several days. He feared he might lose it, and he didn't want to make a big scene. He looked dazed, his voice emotionless. He had no idea if Mom's move was forever. He didn't say bad things about Mom, rather he echoed her phrase that it was "just something she felt she had to do."

Cassie asked "Why?" Dad looked at the floor and shook his head. I angrily blurted out, "Mom loves Becky more than she loves us!" Dad looked up as tears formed in his eyes. Sam went over to hug Dad and started bawling. Cassie joined the two of them on the couch. I wasn't about to cry. I was pissed. Dad seemed to recognize my anger, motioning for me to join them. Nope! I stomped out of the room, out the back door, and down the street.

Within minutes, I was overwhelmed with emotion. My heart felt like it was pounding out of my chest. I started to sweat like crazy. I was dizzy and light-headed. I was breathing like I just ran a race. Leaning against a tree, I slowly sank to the grass. I don't know how long I sat there but luckily my body gradually began to feel more like normal. That was scary. I'd never experienced anything like that before. I knew I couldn't sit there forever, so I headed back.

Dad was washing dishes as I entered the back door. He paused and looked at me. Neither of us had to say a word. I walked over, picked up a towel, and started drying. When we finished, we sat across from each other at the kitchen table. Dad apologized for everything that had happened. I reached for his hand, telling him that he had nothing to be sorry for. I wasn't upset with him. Everything was just a mess. My anger was being replaced with feeling lost. Mom and Dad seemed happy together. Sure, date-nights rarely occurred anymore, but things change. No big arguments. I hadn't heard Dad say anything negative about her time teaching yoga or going out with her friends in ages. I just didn't get it. I went to my room thinking that Dad knew more about this than he was sharing. I was glad we had had a little time with only the two of us. That night, I wondered what Dad was going through. How was he going to work and keep the house going with three kids by himself?

Dinner

On Thursday Mom called inviting us to her place – no, really Becky's place – for dinner on Saturday. After taking the call, Cassie immediately came looking for me. I really didn't know what to say. Neither of us wanted to go, but we knew we couldn't say no. It had been less than a week since Mom left, and I don't believe anybody had come close to adjusting to the change. My feelings were a jumbled mess. One moment I'd be angry, next sad, always confused and overwhelmed. I feared I might break down and screw up the whole dinner. Cassie seemed to be doing a better job of pushing the whole mess out of her mind. I tried but couldn't. I had trouble sleeping and didn't have much of an appetite. I had always been a good student, but the last few days I found myself having difficulty completing any schoolwork. Everything just sucked!

Mom picked us up at 5:00 Saturday evening. She asked a few questions about our week, but quickly gave up after a bunch of one-word responses. Mom quickly realized that we were all uneasy about the dinner, driving in silence the remainder of the ride. When we arrived, she did not immediately get out of the car. She turned to us, saying that moving out was the hardest decision she had ever made. She confessed that she wasn't even sure it was the right choice. She recognized how unsettling it had been for all of us, hoping that we could be patient with her. Becky was probably as nervous about having us over for dinner as we were about coming. Mom felt we would really grow to like Becky if we gave her half a chance.

Becky met us at the door and was all smiles. Mom was right, Becky displayed a nervous smile if I'd ever seen one! They had snacks in the living room and several games on the coffee table. Nobody really knew what to say. There were a couple of awkward questions about our week, followed by Becky retreating to the kitchen to finish fixing dinner. Mom nodded to us saying we were doing fine. Luckily within minutes we all headed to the kitchen for spaghetti and Texas Toast. Sam is kind of a slob when eating spaghetti. Actually, that turned out to be a good thing, as laughing at his eating habits sort of broke the ice. We had brownies and chocolate chip ice cream for dessert. I realized that Mom had picked out our favorites for dinner. She was trying. I guess they both were trying.

After dinner we played Uno. Playing a game was a good idea. We were able to avoid talking, which still felt uncomfortable. Sam appeared to be adapting better than Cassie and me. I noticed Mom and Becky grinning and nodding to each other several times throughout the evening. Becky appeared more at ease by the time we headed home.

Everyone was still very quiet on the ride home. Mom thanked us as she turned off the car. She realized that it had been difficult for everyone and hoped we would be able to visit again soon. Sam gave an enthusiastic yes. Cassie and I nodded as we got out of the car. Sam asked if Mom was coming in to see Dad. "Maybe next time."

Dad was watching TV when we arrived home. Thankfully, he didn't ask anything about how it went. It was late so we all headed off to bed. I laid in bed that night, not sure how I felt about our evening with Becky and Mom. Becky seemed like a nice person, although a cloud of uneasiness hung over the evening. This was the first time we'd ever had the opportunity to talk with her, even though we'd met her several times. Why was Mom there? That was the nagging question I couldn't ignore. It was driving me nuts!

Adapting

Things at the house had to change. Dad, the non-stop insurance salesman, pretty much eliminated his evening hours so he could be home with us. Cassie and I learned to do laundry and helped more with cleaning. Dad quickly realized that we couldn't only live on heat-it-up food, so he slowly learned to fix a few dishes. Cassie often helped.

From what I could tell, Dad and Mom talked several times a week on the phone. I never heard them argue. Occasionally Mom came in the house when bringing us home. Although friendly with each other, Dad seemed sad, often retreating to his room or his garage workshop when she left.

One evening I entered the kitchen to find Dad sitting by himself staring off into space. I had come down to get something to drink. Dad just shook his head when I offered him a drink. We sat across from each other in silence for like five minutes. I finally broke the silence, remarking that he hadn't seemed like himself since Mom moved out. Dad sort of half grinned.

From there, our conversation drifted to how things had changed around the house without Mom.

Eventually, I worked up the guts to ask what happened. Dad's shoulders slumped as he said he had no idea. He had thought things were pretty good at home. He brought up our recent vacations out West. I frustratingly said something about how Mom and her yoga had ruined our family. She wouldn't have met Becky if she hadn't done the yoga thing. Dad shook his head saying that it was something more than yoga. I didn't get it. What else could it be? Things started to change after Mom became a yoga instructor and hung out more with her yoga friends.

Dad noticed that I was becoming more upset. He leaned across the table, took my hands saying we were still a family, whether Mom lived with us or not. I remember looking in his watery eyes, wondering if he really believed what he had just said. Sure, four of us were still a family, but where did that leave Mom? She'd been gone for several months, and we had learned to live with it. I guess we were slowly adapting. We really didn't have a choice. Mom was still our mom but was becoming less and less a part of the family with each passing day. We both realized that we had been talking for nearly an hour. It was a school night, and I was up way too late.

When I entered our bedroom, Cassie asked where I'd been. I told her I had run into Dad in the kitchen. She persisted in questioning why it took so long. I told her we chatted for a while. Cassie wanted to know what about. "Just stuff." She gave up and rolled over. I laid in bed pondering my talk with Dad. I didn't realize he was hurting so bad. I guess he missed Mom a lot more than he let on. Was he enjoying anything in life? Again, I got the feeling that he knew more than he shared.

Soccer

Mom made it to most of our sporting and school events. She usually sat with Dad and Sam. It kind of seemed as if nothing had changed. We all chatted, laughed, and even went out for pizza together once. The major difference was that Mom took off in her car as we left in Dad's.

All of that changed one Saturday when Becky came with Mom to Cassie's soccer game. They approached us on the sidelines with their chairs. Dad turned, his face becoming red as he spotted them. I didn't know what to expect. He nodded and stared at the field not saying a word for the remainder of the half. If you knew Dad, you'd have recognized something was wrong. Dad never kept quiet at a soccer game. Mom tried talking, but he stared at the game, saying nothing. I was afraid that there might be a scene with Dad blowing his cool. He gave several other parents the cold shoulder when they came up to talk at half time.

Eventually, he headed to the parking lot saying that he wasn't feeling well. I sat quietly watching him head off. Sam was kicking a ball with several kids, not even noticing Dad's departure. Awkward, awkward, awkward! I don't think Becky said a thing up to that point. Mom tried talking to me, but I was not in the mood to talk. I'm not sure what I was in the mood for. I just wanted to get the game over and head home. Why did Mom have to show up with her? Didn't she think at all about how Dad might feel, about what other parents might think?

Cassie came across the field to join us after the game. She was unaware that anything happened. She immediately asked about Dad. Mom said that he was not feeling well and sat in the car for the second half. I rolled my eyes as she looked at me. Becky quickly folded their chairs while suggesting that they needed to get going. Mom said she'd call as the two of them quickly headed to their car. Cassie looked at me again as if expecting me to tell her what was going on. Shaking my head, I said, "Dad's waiting in the car."

Dad apologized to Cassie for not seeing the second half of the game. He indicated that he was okay when Cassie asked how he was feeling. She looked at me as I mouthed, "Later." Sam was the only one who spoke on the ride home. Cassie met me in our room after showering. I filled her in on what had happened at the game.

After dinner Dad sat down with Cassie and me. I was shocked about how open he was with us. Dad sadly expressed how he was not sure if Mom would ever return home. He missed her as much as we did. I think he saw himself as a failure. His wife moved out for another woman. That's not normal, is it? Dad kept repeating how important we were to him and that he would never leave us. Neither Cassie nor I asked the "why question." We both wondered if Dad had any answers.

That night Cassie sat on the side of my bed looking real serious. She had been wondering for the last several weeks if Mom liked women more than she liked men. At first, I didn't understand what she was saying. Cassie asked if I'd heard of the word "lesbian." Sure, I'd heard it, but I can't say I knew much about lesbians. Cassie went on to explain that several weeks ago she had realized Mom had never shown us her bedroom at Becky's. She had done a little snooping on a trip to the bathroom while visiting. She discovered only one room with a bed, the other room looked like an office. I didn't know what to say. Cassie had also noticed Mom and Becky exchanging little glances and smiles the way Mom and Dad had done in the past. My head started spinning. I was starting to feel ill. Were Mom and Becky more than just good friends? I didn't know what that all meant. I just wanted to close my eyes, fall asleep and wake up tomorrow with everything the way it had been, Mom, Dad and three kids. Still awake around 2:00, I whispered Cassie's name. We both were awake. I wasn't alone.

Discovering the Truth

Even though it had been several months, neither Cassie nor I had told any of our friends about Mom moving in with Becky. What was I supposed to tell my friends? I didn't understand any of it. I figured that Mom would soon miss us more than she enjoyed living with Becky and move back home. When they showed up together for the game, my hopes began to fade. I was hounded by the question: why Becky? Weren't we good enough?

I couldn't get the idea of Mom being a lesbian out of my head. I googled lesbian and there were sites for lesbian organizations and support groups but there also were a bunch of pictures and videos. I was shocked as I stared at them. I heard footsteps in the hall and quickly clicked off. The problem was, I had trouble getting those images out of my head. Did Mom kiss Becky? Did Mom and Becky take their clothes off together? Gross!

I asked Connie, my best friend, if she knew anything about lesbians. She stopped in her tracks, giving me a really strange look. Why, did I think I might be a lesbian? I assured her that was not the case. I told her that I had seen a movie on Netflix where several characters were lesbians, and I was curious. Connie didn't know anything more than I did.

I don't know why, but I needed answers. Mom was still my mom, and I would always love her, but I needed to know. Cassie and I had spoken several more times and she believed that Mom and Becky were lovers. She gave a long list of reasons for believing this; however, she never confronted Mom. It just was all so unbelievable. I thought about asking Dad, but that was too weird. I knew he was upset and I didn't want to make things worse.

As weeks passed, questions and images of Mom and Becky would not leave my head. One Sunday Mom took me out shopping. Sitting at the ice cream shop, I just blurted out my questions. I think Mom was shocked by my bluntness. Mom paused before answering. She said she loved Becky very much. Her feelings for Becky started when they took yoga instructor training together. Mom said she tried to deny her feelings, but eventually they won out. She still cared for Dad but couldn't be with him anymore. She had wanted to talk to us kids for ages but was scared we might hate her if we learned the truth. I asked if Dad knew. Mom slowly nodded. We sat talking for a while longer as our ice cream melted.

Coming Months

Now that I knew the truth, what was I supposed to do with it? I wanted to tell my friend Connie but feared what she might think. I could not hold it in any longer. I told her everything. She got a puzzled look, asking if that was why I questioned her about lesbians several weeks ago. I didn't deny it. I felt embarrassed. Thank God, Connie was cool with it. She didn't ask a bunch of dumb questions. Connie gave me a hug, saying it must be hard, but it wasn't my fault, and everything would be all right. I wasn't even sure what "all right" meant anymore.

One day on the playground, Stanley, the class jerk, came up yelling that he heard my mom liked kissing girls. I was completely taken by surprise, not knowing how to respond. He wanted to know if I liked kissing girls too. I turned to walk away as my eyes filled with tears. Stanley followed me saying all sorts of things about Mom and me. Several classmates noticed, but they just stood there watching, doing nothing. Connie, who was across the playground, ran over and planted herself in front of Stanley, not saying a word, just staring him in the eye. I don't think a girl had ever stood up to him before. He immediately backed off, mumbling to himself as he retreated. What a wuss! What an asshole! Connie put her arm around me, telling me everything would be okay. Some of our classmates who witnessed the whole event, just stood there, expressionless.

Stanley's remarks got me thinking. How many other classmates knew Mom lived with a woman? Did they think my mom was a lesbian? Yeah, you heard me: I believed Mom was a lesbian. So what? It actually felt good to admit what I had been wondering for months. Mom as much as told me at the ice cream shop. She just hadn't used the word. Up till now, I hadn't been able to say the word "lesbian." I had to face reality. I still wondered if kids might treat me differently? Would boys ever like me, or would they think I might be like my mom?

As the next several months wore on, it became more obvious that Mom was never coming home. I noticed that she and Becky displayed more signs of affection between them on our visits. One Sunday Mom suggested that we go to a local park for a music and craft festival. This was the first time we ventured into public with Mom and Becky. I felt a little weird. Several times I noticed them holding hands. I didn't know what to make of it. It was hard enough seeing them touching in their house. Even though I didn't know anyone at the festival, I felt like everyone was looking at us. Cassie rolled her eyes several times when I looked at her. Nothing appeared to bother Sam. I kind of wished I could be like him.

All Things Come to An End

Mom had been living with Becky for over a year now. We visited every other weekend and occasionally saw them during the week. Sometimes she stopped in and talked to Dad when bringing us home. I never head them argue. Over time, Dad was less unhappy after she went back to her place. He gradually seemed to accept Mom and Becky showing up to sporting and other events. I had to believe some of my friend's parents already figured out what was going on. Luckily, they never asked anything about it. I'm not sure what I would have said.

I forced myself to become more informed about LGBT issues. I'd like to think I was an openminded, accepting kid; however, those were other people, not my mom! Was she always a lesbian and just didn't know, or did she somehow turn into one? How do you turn into a lesbian after you marry and have three kids? If she could turn into a lesbian as an adult, could I? I began to question myself every time I complimented a girl on a cute outfit or haircut. Was I noticing girls too much? God, I hated this! Why did she do this to us?

Becky was out shopping one Saturday when we visited. As we sat at the table after lunch, Mom informed us that she and

Dad were getting a divorce. Sam looked puzzled. Cassie and I looked at each other as a tear began to run down my cheek. Mom realized several months ago that she wanted to spend the rest of her life with Becky. She loved us today as much as she did the day we were born. She would always be our mom and would always be a part of our lives. Mom still cared for Dad, but things had changed. It was time to move on.

That night in bed I think I felt a sense of relief. Sure, I wished none of this stuff with Mom and Becky had happened, but it did. However, I didn't cause it, Cassie didn't cause it, Sam didn't cause it, and God knows, Dad didn't want any of this to happen. I repeatedly told myself that I had to give up the "why" question, but that was a hard thing to do. I kept telling myself it just didn't matter, Mom was happier, Dad was becoming happier, and Cassie, Sam and I, well, we had adjusted. I didn't cry in bed the night of Mom's announcement, but I didn't sleep much either. I think in some ways I was just ready to move on.

Today

I finally started calling where Mom lives "their place," not "Becky's place." It still feels weird, but that's just the way it is. Dad never says anything bad about Mom or Becky. They continue to talk and are both flexible about anything involving us kids. If you didn't know what had happened, you'd think they were just good friends. We have our own routines at home. Dad is always home in the evenings and actually appears to be enjoying life more. He and Sam started fishing together. It's created a special bond between them. We were also talking about out next big vacation.

By now my friends and their parents know what had happened. For the most part, everyone has been very accepting and supportive. Although no one is overly friendly to Mom and Becky, no one is rude either. Everyone pretty much acts as if nothing unusual had happened in my family. I am relieved. I guess I am lucky.

To this day I am still haunted by the "why" question. I joined a teen divorce group at my school to try to find some answers and feel some support. I never realized that there are so many crazy family situations. There is alcoholism, adultery, physical and emotional abuse, abandonment, drug use and much more. I guess my story isn't as unique as I thought it was.

Afterword

While this is a work of fiction, the old adage "write what you know" is what brings these stories to life. The situations are my creation, but as I said in the Introduction, the inspiration comes from the amazing and resilient young people who have shared their lives, their feelings, and their fears with me. In my capacity as both a school psychologist and counselor, I have facilitated many different programs for students. Some of my programs encouraged leadership and relationship building, like the Peer Mediation and the Kindness Project. I led groups for children of substance abusers, groups where they were substance abusers themselves, groups for students that had behavior issues or had given up on school or maybe even on themselves, and groups for children of divorced, separated or single parent families.

Although I do individual counseling, I think I have had the most success in the group setting, especially with students of non-traditional families. Repeatedly, students have said things like, "Now I don't feel so alone," or "I thought I had a crazy situation, other kids have it way worse than me." And maybe, most importantly: "I learned so much from the other kids in our group." We usually think of peer pressure as a negative thing, but over my career I've come to recognize that the "power of the group" can create very positive outcomes.

I have worked with all age groups, from preschool through high school, but the majority of my career has been spent with middle or junior high school students. We are all aware of the usual challenges for this age group, rapid physical changes, balancing the increased responsibilities of home and school, with increased freedom and independence, and dealing with the ever evolving, and frequently revolving social circle. There are too many questions, and too few answers. One day grown-ups, especially their parents, will treat them like third graders, and the next day expect them to act like adults. Feelings often run raw and change like the flip of a switch. Parents are geniuses one day, and idiots the next. Friends are everything, and conversely, lack of friends is devastating.

Insecurity rules the day. Young people often hide behind masks, and while some will embrace their uniqueness, maybe even flaunt it, most will do everything they can to fit in, including hiding what they really like or how they really feel. Add separation or divorce into the mix and all the typical upheaval of this time is intensified. Often parents and/or the students have reservations about the group setting. Parents may fear that they will be disparaged, or family secrets will be shared, and students may fear removing their masks, of letting their peers finding out their truths.

So how does "the group" work? It starts off slowly. Boundaries, trust and relationships must be established, not only between the student and the facilitator, but between all the members of the group. Gradually, through shared experiences, the students will be guided to a better understanding of their feelings, and the introduction of coping skills. Tears often flow freely, as the group is often the first place a student has the courage to open up about family situations. While some will gush with emotion, others will sit back and observe. Most will eventually become comfortable enough to share at least some of their story.

Discussions cover a wide range of topics. Students complain that they feel like a rope in a tug-of-war, with each parent pulling an arm, or they feel like a mailman delivering messages between parents, or a pawn in a game of one-upmanship. Parent infidelity is often an awkward topic. Most students are uncomfortable with their parents dating, or a boyfriend or girlfriend moving in, especially if the break-up was recent. These kids are just learning to deal with their own relationships with the opposite gender, which is confusing enough on its own.

Family finances take on a new dimension, and things that were once taken for granted may no longer be affordable, or downsizing may occur. Stepparents often blur lines of authority, and step-siblings can redefine "sibling rivalry." It's not unusual for alcohol or other substance abuse to play a role in the family dynamics. Legal concerns such as visitation, custody and even restraining orders now become part of their vernacular. "Shared Parenting," while it sounds like a positive, often creates difficulties as everyone tries to navigate the needs of the family members and their increasingly busy schedules.

While I ask questions, offer suggestions, or gently redirect discussions, it's the participants themselves who offer a validation of feelings, or the deepest insights, and sometimes even the best advice or viable solutions. Another bonus, it's rare that new friendships among group members don't occur. The stories in this book are a continuation of the group process. Hopefully they have provided a validation of feelings or insights into family dynamics, but most importantly, that they have provided encouragement to seek out assistance from school professionals or other trusted adults such as grandparents or church leaders.

To the parents, I would like to add a few additional comments. As noted in the Introduction, some relationships have to end. If your separation or divorce is recent, you are faced with this new reality. You may be experiencing a roller coaster of emotions, from anger and abandonment to grief and guilt. Possibly you are overwhelmed with legal challenges or financial difficulties. Like they advise you in an airplane: "secure your own oxygen first," then your child's. Prioritize your needs and take it one step at a time. It might be the first time you ever needed a lawyer or an accountant. You may want to seek counseling or a support group for the same reasons your child should. At the least, find a family member or friend you can confide in. Don't be afraid to ask for help.

Having said that, don't let your child's oxygen get lost in the chaos. Don't be so blinded by your own needs that you fail to recognize what's going on with your child(ren). Communication and honesty are crucial, and including them in the decision process, when appropriate, can be helpful. You'll have to find a balance between not keeping them in the dark and TMI!

Maybe the break-up was a while ago and your child(ren) were too young to remember or understand what occurred at the time. Initially they seemed to adapt, but as teens they are looking at things from a new perspective. Family issues like visitation or shared parenting may not have been an issue at age six, but they are a big deal at age thirteen. And almost every child holds on to the hope that their parents will get back together, even if significant others are involved. Try to put yourself in their shoes. You've been their age, but they haven't been yours, so their perspective is not as wide.

This collection is just a sampling of the types of stories I've heard in my long career. While I created some difficult situations on these pages, they only begin to scratch the surface of some of the heartbreak and turmoil that these young people have endured. I hope that I have in some way, no matter how small, helped them navigate through these difficult moments of their lives. I never cease to be amazed at how resilient, adaptable, generous, and courageous young people can be. They have and continue to provide me with a purpose and a hope for the future.

Acknowledgements

I have always believed that one's achievements are rarely the result of individual effort. The assistance and encouragement of others, whether out in the open or behind the scenes, plays a vital role in one's success.

The writing of *My Name Is...* is no exception. It would not have been possible without a number of individuals. Brandy, Paul, Karen, Bill, Carol, Jeff, Kathy, Tom, Katie, Agata, Jim, Keira and Rylie all served as critical readers. This group includes school psychologists, teachers, authors, a counselor, a social worker, a psychiatrist, and students. They generously committed their time and provided much valued feedback and support. Grace gave of her talents to design the cover. I am eternally grateful to them all.

The individual who deserves my greatest thanks is Cathy, my wife. When asked what she thought after I had finished the first story, she said, "I was late because I wanted to read it from beginning to end, to see if the story flowed and if it had a good ending. Keep writing." Cathy served as my primary editor and idea person. Her constant encouragement during the writing and publishing process kept me going when I occasionally considered hitting the "delete" key.

Made in the USA
Monee, IL
13 June 2024

59356617R00125